CRITICS THINK DORKO IS MAGNIFICENT!

"A YOUNG WOULD-BE MAGICIAN GETS LESSONS IN BOTH STAGECRAFT AND LIFE FROM A CRUSTY ELDER ... THE SUPPORTING CHARACTERS STEAL THE SHOW."
—*Kirkus Reviews*

"SHORT CHAPTERS KEEP THE STORY MOVING. ROBBIE HAS IMPRESSIVE DETERMINATION, BUT IT IS GRANDMA MELVYN WHO IS THE STAR IN THIS MOVING STORY."
—*Booklist*

"SATISFYING AND ENJOYABLE, DORKO WILL ENGAGE RELUCTANT AND VORACIOUS READERS ALIKE."
—*School Library Journal*

"A THOROUGHLY LIKABLE MIDDLE-GRADE NOVEL, OFFERING A BLEND OF POIGNANCY AND GIGGLE-WORTHY HUMOR, THIS BOOK IS A SOLID BACK-TO-SCHOOL READ."
—*Bulletin of the Center for Children's Books*

ALSO BY ANDREA BEATY

NOVELS

Secrets of the Cicada Summer
Attack of the Fluffy Bunnies

PICTURE BOOKS

When Giants Come to Play
Iggy Peck, Architect
Rosie Revere, Engineer
Happy Birthday, Madame Chapeau

DORKO
the MAGNIFICENT

ANDREA BEATY

AMULET BOOKS
NEW YORK

The Library of Congress has catalogued the hardcover edition of this book as follows:

Beaty, Andrea.
Dorko the magnificent / Andrea Beaty.
pages cm
ISBN 978-1-4197-0638-7 (hardback)
[1. Magicians—Fiction. 2. Magic tricks—Fiction. 3. Grandmothers—Fiction. 4. Family life—Fiction. 5. Humorous stories.] I. Title.
PZ7.B380547Dnn 2013
2012045674

ISBN for this edition: 978-1-4197-1019-3

Text copyright © 2013 Andrea Beaty
Illustrations copyright © 2013 Nathan Hale
Book design by Meagan Bennett

Printed and bound in U.S.A.
10 9 8 7 6 5 4 3 2 1

Amulet Books are available at special discounts when purchased in quantity for premiums and promotions as well as fundraising or educational use. Special editions can also be created to specification. For details, contact specialsales@abramsbooks.com or the address below.

THE ART OF BOOKS SINCE 1949
115 West 18th Street
New York, NY 10011
www.abramsbooks.com

TO RAY, JOSEPHINE, ROY, AND ESTEL.
MAGNIFICENT, ALL.

PROLOGUE

I HAVE A QUESTION FOR YOU. YES, I'M TALKING TO YOU. I KNOW THAT MOST writers don't do that, but I don't care. I'm going to talk directly to you because I'm a magician and magicians always talk to their audiences. It's how we make our audience more comfortable. Plus, it's more fun that way.

So here's my question: What do they call that moment after something happens but before anyone knows how to react? You know the one I'm talking about: when time stands still for a single heartbeat and anything is possible. Sometimes it's after something good and sometimes it's not. But for that one moment, anything can happen. Anything at all. I'm pretty sure that moment has a name, because anything so important has to, doesn't it?

I know a lot about that moment, because it comes right after my magic trick and just before I say, "Ta-daaaa!" When there's still the chance that everyone will be amazed and yell "Bravo!" and clap or at least not laugh or scream or call the fire department. Again.

You've probably felt that moment, too. Like right after you open a book and just before you read the first line. Before you know if a book stinks and you have to change the characters' names to "Lipzilla" and "Sir Tidy Diaper" so you don't die of boredom. And by the way, if you feel the need to change my name—which is Robbie Darko—to get through this book, knock your socks off. I'd change it myself if I could. And someday, I just might. Though I would *not* pick Sir Tidy Diaper, for your information. I'd pick a mysterious-sounding Russian name like Vladislov Kanzinzki. It sounds better than Dorko, which is what everyone calls me now, thanks to Mr. Nate Watkins, fifth-grade loser.

So if you know what they call that moment I'm talking about, I hope you'll tell me. I've been wondering about it since last year's talent show, which stunk. And, no, I will not go into details. I will tell you that my act involved a salamander named Sir Isaac Newt, a baseball cap, and Principal David Adolphus. I performed my trick perfectly, and then that moment with no name arrived, and I held my breath for a single heartbeat, and just before I said, "Ta-daaaa!" Principal Adolphus revealed his phobia of salamanders *and* his ability to scream like a first-grade girl. I didn't know that Principal Adolphus had amphibia-phobia. Did you?

So last year's talent show stunk, but that's old news. Stale cheese. I'm in fifth grade now, and I'm going to come up with a great new act for this year's show. One that will leave Hobson Elementary School talking about me long after I graduate.

Oh. One last thing. If you're reading this book to find out how magic tricks work, go find a book about some jerk named Sir Tidy Diaper who spoils surprises for everybody, because you're reading the wrong story.

CHAPTER 1

THE HARDEST PART ABOUT WRITING A TRUE STORY IS MAKING YOUR LIFE SOUND exciting. I want my story to be like an action movie, but it's harder than you'd think. My book can't include explosions, because fireworks are illegal here. It can't have car chases, because I won't drive until I'm sixteen. (Or thirty, if Dad reads that last sentence.) It can't even include an alien invasion, even though my brother is weirder than E.T. But don't worry, because someday someone will turn my book into an action movie with car chases, exploding aliens, and sound effects! Since I know that's going to happen in the future, I'm just going to write what really happens for now. I'll start with Mom's birthday party. By the way, if you want to add sound effects, go ahead. I might add some, too! *Kaboom!*

Sunday was Mom's birthday, and I had the perfect present for her. A magic trick. It's more of a parlor trick than a magic one, but it's cool. It's the trick where I pull a tablecloth off the dining room table without moving a single dish. I've been working on it for weeks. Since I wanted to surprise Mom, I only practiced when she was working late at the loan company. I got a lot of practice.

The tablecloth trick needs a hemless tablecloth. I found a fancy red tablecloth in the dining room drawer, but it had a thick hem, so I fixed it with Mom's sewing shears. I know what you're thinking, that Mom wouldn't like me using her expensive sewing shears, but it's okay. She doesn't need them, because she hasn't sewn anything since she started working again. Not even my Halloween costume.

Sunday morning, Mom sat at the kitchen table with a giant stack of files, an adding machine, and a cup of coffee. Dad was on a plane coming home from somewhere, but I don't remember where. Dad is kind of like Waldo. He travels so much, I never know where he is. I *did* know that he was going to pick up dinner for the party when he landed. It was Mom's special day, so we didn't want her to cook or anything like that.

Aunt Trudy was even buying the cake. My brother and I would take care of everything else.

"Happy birthday!" I said. "I have a big surprise for your party!"

"I'm sure it will be great," Mom said without looking up.

"It will!" I said. "You'll see."

"I'm terrible for saying this, but I wish we weren't having company," she said. "I've got to get through all these cases by tomorrow."

"Don't worry," I said. "We'll do everything."

That got her attention.

"Oh," she said, but not in a good way.

"Dad's picking up Schwartzman's!" I said. "It's your favorite."

"It is," she said. "But we just can't swing the expense right now."

"It's your birthday," I said. "We have to do something special."

She smiled a little, but she looked a little worried, too.

"Relax, Mom!" I said.

"Uh-huh," she said. "Just keep it simple and use paper plates so there won't be any mess."

"No!" I said. "We have to use the good dishes."

I couldn't tell her that I needed the good dishes for my trick. Paper plates are too light and would be dragged off the table. They would ruin the whole trick.

"No, Robbie," she said. "I don't have time to dig out the good dishes."

"I'll do it," I said. "I'll clean up, too. Please?"

Mom looked at the mountain of files in front of her. She waved her hands at me.

"Okay . . . fine," she said. "Just don't break anything. And help Harry clean the family room. He's got bubble gum wrappers all over the place again."

I started toward the door.

"Hold on," she said. "We need to talk about something else."

"In a minute," I said, and ran out of the room before she could change her mind about the dishes.

I know when to make a fast getaway.

(Note to future movie producers: You have my permission to change my exit to a high-speed car chase, if you want. You're welcome.)

CHAPTER 2

I RAN INTO THE FAMILY ROOM, WHERE MY SIX-YEAR-OLD BROTHER, HARRY, was climbing on the back of the couch. I call him Ape Boy because he climbs on everything, just like an ape. He also chews on anything that gets near his mouth. Pencils. Legos. Fingers—not just his own. You name it. Last week, he chewed through the strap on the new messenger bag Mom bought for work. She got so mad she almost cried.

The doctor suggested giving Harry bubble gum, so Mom bought a bucket of it. Now he chews on everything *and* sticks gum on it, too. The doctor says he'll outgrow it, but I doubt it.

Ape Boy sat on the back of the couch, chewing on the TV remote *and* a wad of bubble gum at the same time. There were a thousand bubble gum wrappers on the floor. He drops them everywhere, which is why Ape Boy is *not* allowed in my room. Ever!

"Clean up this mess, Ape Boy!" I said.

"Don't call me Ape," Harry said.

"Don't act like one. And get busy. We're having company."

"I don't want company."

"Don't you want Mom to have a good party?" I asked.

"Yeah."

"Then stop being a baby and just do it."

"I'm not a baby!"

"I know," I said. "You're an ape!"

I whacked him with one of the couch pillows, and he fell onto the couch seat laughing. He grabbed the other pillow and whacked me back. That was the beginning of the Epic Battle of the Family Room. (Insert movie explosions here: *Kerblooey! Kerblam!*)

The Epic Battle of the Family Room lasted until Mom yelled from the kitchen.

"Get busy! They'll be here in an hour."

"We are!" I yelled back and hit Ape Boy again.

After that, I fixed the cushions and straightened

up the magazines while Ape Boy stored the bubble gum wrappers under the couch. He was happy because he'd found some old Reese's Pieces and popcorn from the last Movie Night Mom and I'd had. The popcorn was covered with carpet fuzz, and the candy was old and really nasty, but Ape Boy didn't care. Like I said, he chews *everything*. (Which is the other reason Ape Boy is not allowed in my room. Ever! My room is an Ape-Boy-free zone. And that's how I like it.)

I love Movie Night. Since Dad and Ape Boy hate old movies, it's just me and Mom and a big bowl of popcorn with Reese's Pieces. It's the best combination ever: A little salty. A little sweet. A lot awesome. It's funny how Mom and Dad are alike and different, too. They both love hot peppers and baseball, but Dad loves new movies with explosions and Mom loves old movies with dancing. Maybe someone should make a movie with dancing *and* explosions. A movie like that would have some pretty weird sound effects. *Tap-tap-kaboom!*

I started watching old movies with Mom when I was a little kid. When Fred Astaire and Ginger Rogers danced around in their fancy clothes, Mom picked me up and twirled around the room until we got dizzy and fell on the couch laughing. I think Mom would have been a movie star if she'd lived back then. She has a way of standing out. I like that.

Those old-time movie stars made people watch them even when they weren't dancing. They stood out. Sometimes when I do magic, I think that maybe I do, too. Just a little.

For the record, I like movies where things explode, too. But I love watching the old movies with Mom, just me and her. We used to have Movie Night every Friday, but that was before Dad lost his good job and Mom had to start her bad one. Mom says we'll have another Movie Night soon. Probably next week . . . maybe.

Just in case, I bought a big box of Reese's Pieces and made Mom hide them so I won't eat them if she has to cancel. Again. One time, I heard Principal Adolphus say that the more things change, the more they stay the same. I don't know what he was talking about. The more things change, the more things stink.

When we were done cleaning, Ape Boy climbed onto the back of the couch again and unwrapped a new piece of bubble gum. He threw the wrapper onto the floor, but I didn't care. I had a table to get ready.

I put the red tablecloth on the dining room table

and got Mom's good china from the cabinet. I set the whole table just like Mom does. I even put out the tall beeswax candles that Mom keeps for very, very special occasions. I knew Mom wouldn't mind. What's more special than your own birthday? Especially when your present is a magic trick?

You might wonder why I went through so much trouble to make the table so fancy. I have two reasons. The first one is about science. (Lots of magic is about science, which is why I actually do okay in science class.) Mom's fancy dishes are super heavy and push down on the table with more force than the tablecloth has when I jerk it away from the table. That's why the dishes stay right where they started.

The other reason is about drama. (Magic involves a lot of drama, which is why I would also do okay in acting class, if my school was smart enough to have one.) Using the fancy dishes adds danger. Who cares if I knock over some paper cups and plastic plates? Nobody. But if I goof up and destroy Mom's best china, there will be danger. *Lots* and *lots* of danger. And probably some hiding out in my friend Cat's tree house for a few days. And weeks of being grounded and probably getting a summer job to pay for the china and—oh boy.

Anyhow. Danger makes people pay attention. It gives them focus. In magic, focus is everything. Remember that. It's important.

I was focusing on the table when Mom yelled for me to come to the kitchen.

"We're having pizza," she said.

"I thought Dad was picking up brisket from Schwartzman's."

"His plane is stuck in St. Louis, and he won't land in time to pick it up for dinner, so we're getting pizza," she said. "Which is another sixty dollars on top of Schwartzman's, which we still have to pay for because it was a special order."

"We can have the brisket tomorrow night!" I said.

"I know, kiddo," Mom said. "We just don't have the extra money right now."

Ape Boy ran into the room and jumped onto a chair. "Pizza!" he yelled.

"Get down, Harry!" Mom snapped. "Go watch the front door so I can talk with Robbie."

Ape Boy jumped off and ran down the hall, yelling, "Pizza! Pizza!"

"Look, Robbie," she said. "We need to talk before Grandma Melvyn gets here."

I didn't like the sound of that.

"Why?" I asked suspiciously.

"Grandma Melvyn's got knee problems and she's trying to get an operation," Mom said.

"So?"

"The insurance company is fighting her and . . . well . . . the thing is . . ."

A familiar buzz erupted from Mom's pocket. She pulled out her cell phone and glanced at the screen.

"Ugh . . . ," she said to me. "I've got to take this. I'll only be a second . . . *No . . . I said forty-two thousand . . . No . . . Hold on . . . Wait . . . Let me look . . .*"

Mom mouthed the words *stay here* while she flipped through the files on the table. I didn't stay for long because two seconds later, Ape Boy ran into the room and jumped up and down like an ape in a banana factory.

"They're HERE!" he yelled. "It's time for the party!"

CHAPTER 3

THE WHOLE FAMILY WAS COMING TO THE PARTY. YOU PROBABLY THINK THAT'S a lot of people, but it's not. We have a small family. Just me, Ape Boy, Mom, and Dad, plus Dad's sister, Aunt Trudy, and her husband, Uncle Pete. Oh yeah, and Grandma Melvyn. It's probably a good idea to warn you about Grandma Melvyn in case you're expecting her to be a sweet little grandma who brings me cookies and milk and knits me cozy blankies. She's not. But if you have an extra grandma like that, I'm interested.

Grandma Melvyn is not even my real grandma. She's not *anyone's* grandma. She's my great-great-aunt, but trust me, it doesn't matter how many "greats" you put in front of her title—there is nothing great about her. Dad started calling her Grandma Melvyn after our real grandma died. I guess he felt sorry for her because she didn't have anyone to call her Grandma.

This might be a good time to point out that feeling sorry for Grandma Melvyn is like kissing a scorpion. You get over the idea real fast. I know that sounds mean, but it's not. All it takes is one look at Grandma Melvyn to understand. She's about as tall as a mailbox and she wears glasses that are two inches thick and make her eyes look as big as baseballs. You can see every vein and every floater and sometimes, when she gets mad, her eyeballs wobble. That is not something you want to see. Trust me.

I once saw her make a nine-year-old cry at his own birthday party. Okay, it was me. But you'd cry, too, if she gave you the Wicked Wobble Eye. Grandma Melvyn never smiles and she *never ever, ever* laughs. Did I mention *never*?

One last thing about Grandma Melvyn. She calls everybody "Trixie." And I mean *everybody*! Keep reading. You'll see what I mean.

When Ape Boy yelled, I ran out of the kitchen and looked out the dining room window. Uncle Pete was trying to help Grandma Melvyn up the sidewalk. Every couple of steps, she pushed him away and waved her cane at him like a fencer with a foil. Then she tottered forward a bit and tilted to the right, then the left and backward, until she looked like she would fall over.

Even through the window glass, I could hear her yell, "Get over here, Trixie! Are you going to let an old lady fall down and die out here in this zoysia wasteland you call a yard? Zoysia? Who plants zoysia?"

Uncle Pete grabbed Grandma Melvyn's arm and helped her for a couple of steps, until she pushed him away and the whole thing started all over again, like some weird modern dance.

Aunt Trudy walked behind them, carrying an enormous lopsided cake on a fancy tray. This was bad. Aunt Trudy was supposed to buy the cake instead of making it. She is the worst cook in the world. She burns everything. (She even burned yogurt one time. Don't ask.) Aunt Trudy walked up the sidewalk holding the unnaturally black cake like it was the greatest thing in the world.

I just hoped it was chocolate.

By the time Grandma Melvyn, Uncle Pete, and Aunt Trudy sat down in the dining room, the pizza arrived. Mom got off the phone and came into the dining room, too. The table was beautiful. The pizza looked cool on the fancy dishes like it was all dressed up for the party. Mom was impressed by the improved tablecloth. She ran her fingers along the edge and shook her head. She was speechless. And she hadn't seen anything yet!

Grandma Melvyn liked the pizza.

"Your cooking has improved, Trixie," she said.

"It's delivery," Mom said.

"Exactly," Grandma Melvyn said. "That meal was only half as poisonous as Trixie's meat loaf."

She threw a suspicious look at Aunt Trudy while she stuffed a pepperoni into her mouth. Mom sighed.

Everything was going great. Even Ape Boy was under control. Every time he put his feet on the seat of his chair and looked like he was ready to climb something, Grandma Melvyn gave him the Wicked Wobble Eye and he slid down in his seat and stared at his shoes.

At last, it was time for Mom's cake and presents. Aunt Trudy put the cake on the table. I stood up and made an announcement.

"Before we sing 'Happy Birthday,'" I said, "I have a special birthday trick for Mom."

Aunt Trudy elbowed Uncle Pete, who glanced at the door and scooted his chair a little closer to it. I think he was trying to get a better view of the trick.

"Oh, Robbie, honey," Mom said. "You don't have to do that."

"Of course I do!" I said. "It's your birthday."

"I know," she said. "Just . . . just . . ."

Mom was so excited about my act, she was actually nervous! I could feel the excitement in the air. Perfect!

"Good luck," Mom said.

"Thanks," said Uncle Pete.

I cleared away the dinner dishes and brought out the gold-rimmed dessert plates. Then I filled all the crystal water goblets except Grandma Melvyn's.

"I have my own," she said as she took out a water bottle and filled her glass.

Then she tapped her cane impatiently on the floor.

"Speed it up, Trixie," she said. "I don't have that many years left, and I don't want to spend half of them waiting for that burnt offering Trixie calls a cake."

Aunt Trudy muttered something under her breath, but I couldn't tell what it was because Uncle Pete cleared his throat right then.

I lit the tall beeswax candles.

"Just one more thing," I said.

I went to the hall closet and pulled out the black

satin cape I had stashed inside it earlier. It was part of the Dracula costume Mom had sewn three Halloweens ago, but it made the perfect magician's cape. I put it on and went back to the dining room. Showtime.

I tapped a crystal water goblet with a table knife.

Ting . . . ting . . . ting . . .

"Ladies and gentlemen!" I said in my most dramatic voice. "In honor of Mom's birthday and to celebrate this most auspicious occasion, I will now perform a trick that will both amaze and delight you!"

I paused for effect. Then I grabbed the edge of the red tablecloth and, with a snap of my wrists, jerked it toward the floor. Like magic, it slid under the gold-rimmed plates and the cake. In a heartbeat, I was standing before the amazed crowd with the cloth in my hands and the bare wood of the table gleaming in the candlelight.

I did it!

I dropped the tablecloth on the floor and raised my hands over my head. Then I leaned over and took the biggest bow of my life.

"Ta-daaaa!"

And that was my first mistake.

CHAPTER 4

ACTUALLY, MY FIRST MISTAKE WASN'T TAKING A BOW, IT WAS STANDING UP again.

On the way up, I hit Mom's water glass . . . which fell over and hit a candlestick . . . which fell over and caught a napkin on fire . . . which made Uncle Pete yell, "Pour on water!" . . . which made me throw a glass of water . . . which was my second mistake.

I don't know what Grandma Melvyn had in her water glass, but it sure wasn't water. When I threw it on the flame, it went *WHOOOSH* and the fire spread across the table . . . which made Aunt Trudy knock Uncle Pete right into the cake . . . which made him knock the cake onto the floor . . . which probably saved us all from food poisoning, but which really took the magic out of the moment.

While Ape Boy climbed the china cabinet to get a better view, Mom got the fire extinguisher and put out the flames. When the smoke cleared, Grandma Melvyn and I were alone in the dining room. I looked out the window to avoid the Wicked Wobble Eye, and that's when I heard the weirdest sound ever. It was a wheezing, honking, snorting sound like a cross between an asthmatic goose and an insane pig. I looked at Grandma Melvyn. Sure enough, she was laughing. Or maybe she was having some kind of fit. It was hard to tell. Her whole body shook and tears streamed down her cheeks. She wheezed and sputtered trying to get her breath between snorts. Her face was bright red and she looked like she was going to fall out of her chair.

Perfect. Grandma Melvyn, the woman who never ever, *ever* laughed, was going to laugh herself to death because of me. I was about to call an ambulance when she stopped and said something that nearly knocked me over.

"Well, Robbie," she said, "your bow needs work, but I've seen worse acts."

"What?" I asked.

"Got cake in your ears?"

"No," I said, "it's just that you never called me by my name before."

"Well, you never did anything interesting before," she said. "Maybe staying here won't be as bad as it looks."

"What?" I asked.

Grandma Melvyn narrowed her eyes and leaned back in her chair. Her mouth curled up on one side in something that wasn't quite a smile.

"Well, well," she said. "Trixie didn't tell you yet, did she? I'm stuck with you bunch of losers."

"What?"

"What? What? What?" Grandma Melvyn snapped. "There something wrong with you? Thomas Edison didn't say 'watt' that much, and he invented the lightbulb. Oh, that's a good one."

She went back to wheezing and snorting while I sat there with my mouth open like the first guy in a sci-fi movie to witness the alien invasion: amazed, confused, and too stupid to run.

Grandma Melvyn poked me with her cane.

"Don't work yourself into a wedgie," she said. "I'm out of here the minute those Trixies at Almetta Insurance chuck up the dough for my knee operation. Sooner, if Trixie stops ordering pizza and goes back to cooking."

Grandma Melvyn stood up and leaned hard on her cane. She shuffled out of the room and down the hall. I heard her yell at Mom in the kitchen: "Make with the ice cream, Trixie! You call this a birthday party?"

I sat there a long, long time before I got up and went to my room.

That night, Mom came to my room. She stood in the doorway with her hand behind her back.

"Hey, kiddo," she said. "I brought you some cake."

Great. There's nothing like a slice of charcoal cake after a gigantic flaming disaster.

Mom pulled a cellophane-wrapped cupcake from behind her back and handed it to me. It was one of those store-bought kind with that waxy chocolate icing and a white squiggle down the middle. I love those cupcakes.

"Dad's getting in late tonight, by the way," she said. "But he's gone again early tomorrow, so he'll call to chat tomorrow night."

I didn't say anything.

"Look, Robbie," Mom said. "I was trying to tell you earlier that Grandma Melvyn has to stay with us for a little while so she can get her knee fixed. She's been with Aunt Trudy and Uncle Pete, but they're going on a long trip on Tuesday and Grandma Melvyn can't stay by herself, so she's coming here tomorrow."

"Tomorrow?"

I frowned. I bet they booked a one-way ticket to Grandma-Melvyn-Isn't-Hereville. Aunt Trudy is a bad cook, but she's not stupid.

"Hey," Mom said, "it's what families do. We all make sacrifices, but we'll get through this like everything else. It will be fine. You'll see. First, we have to—"

"Mom!" Ape Boy screamed from the kitchen. "Get it out of my hair! MOM!"

"Bubble gum," she said. "Robbie, here's the thing. We have to—"

"MOOOOMMM!" Ape Boy screamed again.

Mom gave me a tiny hug.

"We'll talk later," she said.

"MOOOOOOOOOOMMMMMMMMMM!"

"I'm *coming*!" she yelled.

Mom closed the door and was gone. I sat on my bed and looked at the cellophane cupcake. Mom used to pack one in my lunch box every day, before we had a budget for everything. Like Mom says, we all make sacrifices.

With a flick of my wrist, I sent the cupcake flying toward the metal trash can beside my desk. It ricocheted off the desk leg into the basket, landing on a pile of empty juice boxes and crumpled Kleenex.

I flipped off my light and went to sleep.

CHAPTER 5

SCHOOL ON MONDAY WAS BORING WITH A CAPITAL BORING, SO I WON'T DESCRIBE it to you. (I want this book to be a coma-free zone, remember?) I wish I could say that getting home after school was also boring, but that would be a lie. Here's what happened.

I came through the kitchen door. Like always.

I grabbed a juice box from the fridge. Like always.

I walked to my room and opened the door. Like always.

I came face-to-face with Grandma Melvyn sitting on my bed. Like *never ever, ever* before!

Grandma Melvyn was sitting on *my* bed in a fuzzy green bathrobe with a fat blue toothbrush in one hand and a fat blue hairbrush in the other. She looked like a furry frog with glasses. Sparkly sweatshirts from Las Vegas, Atlantic City, and Niagara Falls were scattered over the floor, and a pile of jogging shoes sat on my bed beside her. There were red shoes and blue shoes and purple shoes and green shoes, and they all had some kind of glitter or sequins or flashing lights on them.

What followed next was a big mess of high-pitched screams (from me), a lot of yelling about privacy (from her), and a whole lot of sparkly jogging shoes flying toward me (from guess who).

I dropped the juice box and retreated to the kitchen just as Mom walked in the door with Ape Boy, who was wearing a new crew cut. The gum removal had not gone well.

Ape Boy climbed onto a chair and jumped up and down.

"You're in MY room again!" he yelled. "Yay!"

"WHAT?"

"Get off the chair, Harry," Mom said. "And go to your room."

"OUR room!" he yelled, running past me toward the stairs. "Yay!"

Mom put a bag of groceries on the table. "I was going to pick you up at school and tell you before we got home," she said. "But I had to take a call."

"What's going on?" I asked.

"Well," she said. "You should know—"

"He knows!" yelled Grandma Melvyn.

I turned around. She was right behind me, waving a red running shoe in the air like one of those pitchfork-wielding villagers in a Frankenstein movie.

"Trixie busted in like he owned the place!" she said. "Might as well put a freeway through my room if every Trixie on the planet can come barging in whenever he wants."

She wheeled around to leave, then stopped and waved the shoe again. I ducked but she didn't throw it.

"Thanks for the juice box," she said, and limped back toward my room.

"I'm sorry, Robbie," Mom said.

I'm sure Mom said other things, too. Like how it was a temporary situation and that my bedroom was the only one without stairs so Grandma Melvyn needed it and how Mom needed my help since she was working now and Dad was traveling and blah, blah, blah . . .

I didn't stick around to hear it. I went to the garage, grabbed my bike, and hit the road. I biked around the neighborhood, then I did crazy eights in the parking lot at Sunshine Preschool until I got dizzy. After that, I biked over to Cat's. I didn't know if Cat would be home because I didn't tell her I was coming over. And honestly, even if I had called her, she might get busy doing something else and forget. Sometimes Cat does that. So do I. That's one reason we get along. We don't get mad at each other when we flake out and forget things.

When I turned onto her street, I saw Cat standing on the sidewalk in front of her house. She had a piece of chalk in one hand and a baseball cap in the other. The sidewalk was covered with tally marks.

"Want to help?" she asked. "I'm waving at people to see if they like hats. So far, twelve people waved back when I was wearing my hat and seventeen waved when I wasn't."

"Why?" I asked.

"It's a social experiment," she said. "Research. It might be important someday."

Might not.

Cat likes social experiments. Sometimes she wears two different socks just to see how many people will say something. Or maybe she wears them because she likes wearing different socks. It's hard to tell with Cat. She isn't the kind of person who likes ordinary things like matching socks or peanut butter and jelly sandwiches. (She prefers peanut butter and jelly tacos.) Cat likes things the way she likes them. And if they're a little weird, who cares? I guess that includes her friends. And, yes, that probably includes me.

I sat on the sidewalk while Cat waved at cars. Each time someone waved back, I made a tally mark. In between research, I told her about Grandma Melvyn taking over my room.

"You've been banished," she said. "That's exciting!"

"No, it's not," I said.

"Lots of famous people have been banished," she said. "Like Napoleon. He was banished to an island after he tried to take over Europe."

"At least he didn't have to share a room with Ape Boy."

"Think of it as a social experiment," she said.

"Yeah, right," I said.

Cat had to leave for oboe lessons, so I biked home. On the way, I thought about that tough guy, the emperor Napoleon Bonaparte. He got banished to an island off Italy, which probably had a great view and servants who brought him food anytime he wanted it. And I bet he thought it was the end of the world.

Poor baby.

CHAPTER 6

EVERYONE WAS GONE WHEN I GOT HOME. I WENT UPSTAIRS TO APE BOY'S ROOM, where Mom had already moved my stuff. The room still had bunk beds from last year when Dad lost his job and turned my room into an office. That's when I shared a cell with Ape Boy. I hated it.

It was only supposed to be for a month or two, but it took a long time for Dad to find his new job. We had to cut back on lots of things, like cable TV, which stunk because we had to get movies from the library for Movie Night. They have lots of Barney videos, but when it comes to great old movies, our library stinks.

I guess we didn't have enough money for other stuff, either, like the mortgage bill. Mom started taking twenty dollars to the loan company every week. I heard her tell Dad that the guy there said she shouldn't do that because it wasn't enough for the bank to care about and there wasn't anything he could do to help. Mom went back every week anyway. She never let me go inside and she doesn't know that I saw her through the window. But every week, she stood in the guy's office, holding out a twenty-dollar bill until he took it, and the whole time, she only said one word: *please.*

One day, the guy said that if she was going to come to the office all the time, she should just work there already, and he gave her a job as a secretary. Now she's an assistant loan officer and she works really hard so other families don't have to worry about losing their houses. So they never have to stand there holding out a twenty, saying *please.*

When Dad got the job at the paper company and started traveling, I got my room back and that was a good thing. Rooming with Ape Boy was awful. He climbed and chewed in his sleep. I took the bottom bunk to keep him from climbing up and chewing on my pillow. I was safe from that danger on the bottom bunk, but there was another peril that was even worse. Ape Boy liked to drink a lot of water and he was a deep sleeper, if you know what I'm getting at . . . think about it . . . yeah . . . you got it. Let me just say I'm glad someone invented plastic sheets.

Now Ape Boy is forbidden from drinking anything after eight o'clock at night, but it doesn't matter. There are some things a person doesn't want to risk. Let's just say that the prospect of sharing a room again was *not* a good one. But that didn't matter. Here I was again. My blankets and pillows were already on the lower bunk. My posters of magicians were taped to the wall above Houdi's cage, which sat on the dresser.

Houdi is my rabbit, in case I failed to mention that. He looks like an ordinary rabbit, but he's not. He was just a baby when I found him in our garage last summer. He'd escaped from Mrs. Chang's cat, who I call Mittzilla but Mrs. Chang calls Sweetums or Sugar Baby or something pukey that makes him sound like the most adorable little kitty cat ever, which is such a lie. Mittzilla is a hardened criminal who kills everything he catches and leaves parts of his victims on our porch to impress us. Very classy.

Houdi escaped with just a tiny rip on the tip of his ear, which shows how extraordinary he is. Getting away from Mittzilla was a great escape, so I named him Houdi after Harry Houdini, the greatest escape artist in the history of the world. By the way, in case you didn't know, Harry Houdini gave himself that stage name in honor of Jean Eugène Robert-Houdin, one of the greatest magicians in the history of the whole universe. I know all kinds of facts like that. I think it's important to know the history of magic. It gives a magician a little perspective.

Houdi is smart, and he's a very good listener. And I'm not just saying that because he doesn't talk back—which is more than I can say about most people I know. I can tell Houdi listens by the way he looks at me. You're probably thinking that's the dumbest thing you ever heard, but I don't care. If you saw him, you'd know what I mean.

I took Houdi out of his cage and sat on the bottom bunk petting him. He looked around the room and blinked and twitched his nose. I could tell he hated the room. Just like me.

We were counting the wads of bubble gum stuck to the ceiling when Ape Boy ran in and swung onto the top bunk like an orangutan. He landed on the top mattress with half his body hanging upside down and his face six inches from mine.

"Yay!" he said between chomps of bubble gum. "Watch this."

Ape Boy blew a bubble as big as his face.

I popped it with my finger and it collapsed into a thin pink mask from his eyebrows to his chin.

"Mom!" he yelled as he flipped down from the bunk and ran out of the room.

I know it was mean and I shouldn't have done it, but I couldn't help myself. Besides, getting the gum out of his eyebrows would give him something to do for the next ten minutes that didn't involve annoying me. I got up and put Houdi back in his cage and went to the hallway closet. I found an old navy blue sheet filled with holes (probably from Ape Boy chewing on it in his sleep). Then I went to the garage and dug out some white Christmas lights and some heavy silver tape from Dad's toolbox.

I went back to the room and taped the edge of the sheet along the rail of the upper bunk so that it made a curtain for my bed. It was just like those train sleeper cars in old movies. At least it would have been except for the holes. Thanks, Ape Boy.

Setting the stage is the most important part of a magic act. Details matter. I try to remember that and train myself to pay attention to details in everything I do. I'm not very good at it yet, but I keep trying. That's what separates the wannabes from the real magicians. Not quitting.

Right now, the holes in this sheet were details that mattered, so I got busy. I cut stars out of silver tape and stuck them over the holes on the inside of the sheet and—presto chango!—my crummy navy sheet became a night sky! When I plugged in the string of lights and taped them onto the underside of the top bunk, the effect was complete. From the outside, it looked like a crummy blue sheet taped to a bed, but from my bunk, it became a magical nightscape. Okay, it was still a crummy blue sheet with some silver tape and Christmas lights, but at night it would look cool, and at least I had some privacy. Sometimes you have to use what you've got.

I took Houdi out of his cage again and climbed into my new hideout and scratched him behind his ears the way he likes.

"It won't be that bad," I whispered.

Houdi leaned his ears back just a little and gave me a look. That's the thing about rabbits. They always know when you're lying. Especially to yourself.

CHAPTER 7

THAT NIGHT, AUNT TRUDY CAME BY WITH A SMALL BAG OF PILLS AND STUFF that Grandma Melvyn had left in her car earlier. I think Aunt Trudy was afraid Mom would change her mind about taking in Grandma Melvyn, because she beat it out of here as fast as she could. She rang the doorbell with one hand, knocked with the other, and yelled, "YOO-hoo!" just in case we were in comas and didn't hear all the banging.

When I opened the door, she practically threw the bag at me, waved good-bye, and then, with a puff of smoke and the squeal of tires, Aunt Trudy was gone. It was a vanishing act that would make any magician proud.

I carried the bag to "Grandma Melvyn's room." The

door was wide open, and Grandma Melvyn stood there poking the bed with her cane.

"It has bedbugs," she said.

"It doesn't have bedbugs," I said.

"What are you, an exterminator?" she asked. "It has bedbugs. First the zoysia grass and now bedbugs. Are you out to kill me?"

Whatever.

I set the bag on the dresser. Then I gave my old room one last look, went upstairs to the Hideout, and went to sleep.

The next morning, I had one goal: To get out of the house *without* seeing Grandma Melvyn. Fat chance. Mom heard me at the front door and made me come to the kitchen to say good morning and to get my lunch. Grandma Melvyn was sitting at the table with her arms crossed while Mom tried to get her to take her morning pills.

"If you don't take your meds, your knee will swell," Mom said, holding two red pills on her palm.

"What are you, a fortune teller?" asked Grandma Melvyn.

Mom sighed but Grandma Melvyn grabbed the pills and tossed them into her mouth and swallowed.

"Happy?" she asked.

I grabbed my lunch from the fridge with hopes of sprinting to the door before Grandma Melvyn had a chance to cast her Wicked Wobble Eye on me. I was too slow.

"Where do you think you're going, Trixie?" she asked.

"School," I said.

"Oh boy," she said. "Off to the booger mines to spend the day with a bunch of nose pickers! *That* will be fun."

Ouch. That was mean. But it was kind of true. There is at least one kid in my class—who shall remain nameless and who is *not* me—who is a regular spelunker when it comes to his nose. And if you don't know what a spelunker is, look it up.

Mucus in all its forms is an unavoidable part of fifth grade. Of course, I wasn't about to tell Grandma Melvyn that.

"They're not a bunch of nose pickers," I said.

"Well, you would know."

"Yeah," I said.

Wait a minute. What? Was she calling me a nose picker? I looked at Grandma Melvyn to get a clue, but she wasn't smiling. But then again, she wasn't frowning, either. Whatever.

"Gotta go," I said.

"Hold it, Robbie," said Grandma Melvyn.

She blew her nose into a Kleenex, then held it out to me.

"Throw this away," she said.

I must have looked like Luke Skywalker when he falls into that nasty trash pit in *Star Wars*, because Grandma Melvyn snorted.

"Career alert. Don't go into medicine," she said. "You don't have the guts for it."

She got up with the Kleenex in her fist as I made a dash for the door. I passed the trash can just as Grandma Melvyn tossed the Kleenex. The crumpled white tissue ricocheted off the inside wall of the can, and out of the corner of my eye, I saw—or did I just imagine?—two tiny red pills drop into the mountain of banana peels and bubble gum wrappers below.

CHAPTER 8

SCHOOL. CAN WE TALK ABOUT IT FOR A MINUTE? AS WE'VE ALREADY DISCUSSED, I'm in fifth grade, where mucus in all its forms is a part of everyday life. But I'm not going to talk about that. Also, I'm not going to talk about the corner of the classroom that always smells like a mysterious biology experiment gone horribly wrong. I am going to tell you about school and me.

I'm a good student, no matter what my report card says. My grades just "don't show my potential." A lot of kids get better grades, but so what? That's not a good reason for them to think they're smarter than me.

I try my best to pay attention during class, but sometimes I start thinking about interesting things like . . . well . . . anything else. So I miss out on instructions and deadlines and things like that. You get the picture. But on the good side, school gives me lots of time to think about magic tricks. That's a form of learning, isn't it?

I doodle, which is art. I also think about constructing trapdoors and escape boxes, which is engineering. I used to practice my coin tricks, which *was* physical education for my fingers, until Mrs. M made me stop. She got tired of Nate Watkins diving on the floor every time I dropped a quarter. I told her it wasn't my fault that Nate was greedy, but she didn't care. She's like that. She isn't mean, but she doesn't like anything that she hasn't planned for. You'll see what I'm talking about. Being a magician has taught me that things always go differently than you expect. Something always goes wrong, so you have to plan for things you don't plan on. Expect the unexpected. When you do that, you can eliminate it. Sometimes.

While we're talking about my teacher, this is a good time to tell you that we call her Mrs. M because her name is Mrs. Mortzchinski and she's tired of correcting kids who can't pronounce it. The funny thing about Mrs. M is that she has a terrific Russian name and she hates magic. Sometimes life is not fair.

Most of the kids at school are okay (including

the spelunker). Cat is great, and there are a couple of other kids I hang out with. They seem to get the whole magic thing, but then there are people who don't. Nate Watkins, for example. I don't think I'm giving away any state secrets when I tell you that he is not the sharpest crayon in the box. Brain-wise, he's more like the crayon someone left in a hot car until it melted.

In case you forgot, Nate is the genius who gave me the nickname Dorko. If I was the kind of person who had a nemesis, he would be mine. Of course, I'm not that kind of person. If I was, I'd do it right and have a hidden underwater lair, an army of minions to do my bidding, and a master plan for world domination that would include exiling Nate Watkins to a moon base with *no* video games. I don't have those things. (Though between you and me, I have made sketches in my notebook for a terrific prisoner transport rocket in case I ever get them.)

Anyway, when I got to class Tuesday morning, I set my books on my desk and turned around to talk to Cat, who sits behind me. My elbow hit my math book and—*bam!*—I knocked it right off my desk and onto the floor.

"What's the matter, Dorko?" said Nate Watkins, who sits behind Cat. "Can't make your books fly? Is your wand broken?"

Cat rolled her eyes and made a goofball face to show what she thought of Nate. I just ignored him.

Nate thinks he's the coolest thing ever because he gets whatever he wants and always has every video game in the universe. You know the kind of guy. You probably have one in your class, too. Nate has mousy brown hair and really square teeth, but the guy in your class might have dark hair or be blond and might have pointy vampire-shaped teeth. It doesn't matter how they look. It's how they act that makes them annoying.

Nate is clueless about magic. The sad thing is that he's not the only one. Sometimes I think Mom and Dad don't even get it. Sometimes when I want to do a trick, Mom and Dad look like I'm going to turn them into wombats or something, which could never happen because we don't even have wombats in this part of the world, except at the zoo, and they don't loan them out to fifth graders. Don't ask me how I know that. I just do.

Like I said, people just don't get it. I blame Harry Potter. Don't get me wrong. I love Harry Potter, I do! But because of Harry Potter, everybody thinks magicians are wizards, which is *not* the case. I know that you can tell the difference, but I created the following chart for you to share with clueless people you meet who don't.

WIZARDS	MAGICIANS
Are fictional characters.	Are real people. We are also called illusionists.
Wear robes and have long white beards and pointy hats or scars shaped like lightning bolts.	Look like normal people. Only better.
Make things disappear.	Use illusions to make things *seem* like they disappear.
Go to special schools where they learn magic.	Go to boring schools where they wish they could learn magic.
Fight dragons, trolls, evil wizards, and other freaky imaginary creatures.	Fight the urge to flee on goulash day in the school cafeteria. School goulash is much scarier than fighting trolls, because it's made by trolls, and possibly *with* them. It's hard to tell without eating it. And who wants to do that?
Avoid talking about a certain wizard who shall not be named.	Avoid talking to girls.
	Well, that's not really true. I talk to Cat all the time and she's a girl. And some girls are magicians. I would love to talk to them. So I'll change that to "Avoid talking to non-magician girls who aren't named Cat." For now. Though Mom says I'll change my mind about that in middle school. Shows what she knows.

I learned a long time ago that there wasn't any point in trying to educate Nate Watkins, fifth-grade loser. Of course, clueless people aren't going to listen to you, either. But it might make you feel better knowing some of the facts.

Anyway, I feel like I just told you a lot of important

things, but I didn't tell you anything important that happened at school on Tuesday. Looking back, there was only one really important thing. It happened at the end of the day, when Mrs. M gave us an assignment. Luckily, I was actually paying attention. (Hey, sometimes that happens.)

This was my favorite kind of assignment. A speech. And not some boring speech about some boring famous person or some boring topic like whether school uniforms are good or bad. This was a three-minute how-to speech. Due on Thursday.

I knew immediately what I would do. And it didn't bother me when Mrs. M went through the long list of things we could *not* use in our speeches. Saws . . . amphibians . . . fire . . . peanut butter and socks—don't ask! . . . ropes . . . pudding . . .

I'll spare you the entire list. It went on for a while and everyone watched me the whole time she read it, but I didn't care. I knew exactly what I was going to do, and it wouldn't involve any of those things. I was going old-school. Classic.

I was going to pull a rabbit out of my hat.

CHAPTER 9

THIS MIGHT BE A GOOD TIME TO MENTION THAT I DON'T HAVE A TOP HAT. I KNOW what you're thinking: How could I be a magician without a top hat? I ask myself that every day, and I am saving up to buy one. The truth is that I used to have a top hat. Somebody gave me one for my ninth birthday, but I don't remember who. It wasn't an expensive one or anything, but it was an honest-to-goodness magician's top hat. I felt really bad when it got eaten.

That wasn't the only magic present I ever got for my birthday. I got a magic kit on my fifth birthday. I don't remember who gave me that one, either, but I loved it. It had a cheesy black cape with red satin trim, a plastic wand, and a little cardboard box that made a coin disappear and magically reappear. The coin trick worked twice and the adults at my party clapped and cheered. After that, the quarters got stuck inside and I cried and the adults gave me more quarters to shut me up. That was the day I got hooked on magic.

Since then, I've learned lots of tricks. The traditional kind: pulling silk hankies out of my fist, cutting a dollar bill in half and magically putting it back together, pulling a coin out of someone's ear— that kind of stuff. Though let me give you some advice: Never pull a quarter out of my uncle Pete's ear. He has more hair in there than an Ewok and more wax than the Crayola factory. It's a bad combination.

Since I don't have a top hat, I'm going to cheat and use one of Dad's old fedoras. He won't mind. Well, he might, but he'll be in Shanghai for work, which is almost the same as not minding.

Remember when I said I wouldn't tell you how my magic works? Well, I'm about to make an exception. Since I can't do this trick the traditional way, I won't be revealing any trade secrets, so I think that's okay. I'll tell you what I'm going to do, but you have to promise not to tell anyone. Since I can't see you, I'll assume you agree. If you don't agree, shame on you. Put down my book right now.

CHAPTER 10

STILL HERE? I KNEW YOU WOULD BE.

So here's what I'm going to do: I'm going to very carefully use an X-acto knife to cut an X in the top of Dad's hat. Felt is soft but firm, so it will spring back to its original shape and make the X invisible to anyone who is not holding it. I'm also going to cut a matching X through a thick plastic tablecloth glued to the top of a box. I found the perfect tablecloth. It's really ugly and covered with flowers. It's great camouflage.

Tip: When you are trying to conceal something, distract the audience's eye by using patterns. Random floral prints hide marks and cuts. Geometric patterns give the illusion of distance or dimension.

If I do it right, I can stick my hand through the Xs

and reach into the box. That's where Houdi will hide. When I pull him out, the Xs on the tablecloth and in the hat will close behind him and become invisible. *Ta-daaaa!* Yeah, I know it's cheesy, but I think the trick will still be awesome. Everyone loves to see a rabbit pulled out of a hat. And if it goes really well, I can use this trick for my act in the talent show, which is coming in about four weeks. Okay, it's coming in 23.75 days. But who's counting?

CHAPTER 11

I KNOW YOU'RE BUSY, SO I WON'T BORE YOU WITH THE EVENTS BETWEEN Tuesday and Thursday. Let's just say I spent a lot of time in the Hideout practicing. Practice is the most important part of magic.

I found a box big enough for Houdi and some food. I put holes in the bottom so that I could prop it on something and air could get inside. That way Houdi could breathe while we waited for our turn. That's important, because two hours is a long time for anyone to hold his breath. Even a rabbit.

I cut an X in the hat, then I cut a round hole in the top of the box and glued the cloth over it. Then I cut an X in the cloth right over the round hole. I could reach my hand through the X in the hat and the X in the cloth and pull Houdi right out of the box. That was my plan, and it took a lot of work.

On Thursday morning, I was ready. I put Houdi in the box with lettuce and some apples. I packed up my props and headed to school. I got to the classroom before everyone—including Mrs. M—and put the box in the closet on a bunch of encyclopedias so the air holes on the bottom would have great circulation. I hid the cape, hat, and wand in the coat closet right behind the big plastic lunch bin. Each day, one kid is chosen to collect the lunches and put them in the bin. At noon, a different kid takes the bin out and distributes the lunches. Who was in charge of putting lunches into the bin on Thursday morning? You guessed it. Me. That was no accident. I volunteered as soon as I knew about the speeches. Planning is the most important part of magic. And, yes, I know I told you that practice was the most important part. In magic, there are lots of most important parts. That's what makes it so hard.

Because I was in charge of lunch bins, Houdi could hide in the closet until my speech and nobody would have a clue he was there. Nobody could spoil the trick. In magic, you have to control your environment. That's how you eliminate those unexpected problems.

The two hours from the start of school until my speech

passed so slowly, it was ridiculous. I would have fallen into a coma if I hadn't been busy thinking about my trick. Don't believe me? Here's the agenda. Just try to stay awake:

Announcements from Principal Adolphus: Good boring, students. Blah blah blah boring blah blah blah boring blah.

Math: long division + worksheets = boring.

Spelling: B-o-r-i-n-g. Boring.

Other people's speeches: Four score and seven borings ago . . .

Okay, wake up. The list is over. See what I mean about boring?

At last, it was my turn. I went to the closet and put on my cape and grabbed my hat and wand. I picked up the box and walked to Mrs. M's desk. It felt lighter than it had earlier. Houdi must have eaten all the apples.

"Ladies and gentlemen!" I announced. "Prepare to be amazed and astonished! That's right, folks! Before your very eyes, I'm going to pull a rabbit out of my hat!"

I paused for effect. Always pause for effect. It's . . . effective!

Cat clapped. Nate Watkins smirked. Mrs. M sighed and looked at the clock on the wall. I continued.

"That's right, folks. I'm going to pull a rabbit out of this ordinary hat."

I showed them the inside and outside of Dad's fedora to prove it was ordinary. The X was invisible to anyone who didn't know it was there. I tapped the hat with my wand three times and placed it upside down on the cloth-covered box.

"Abracadabra!" I said.

I reached into the hat, through the Xs into the box, and grabbed . . .

A chewed-up apple?

I smiled at the audience. If something goes wrong in an act, you should always smile. The worse it gets, the bigger you smile. It calms the audience. Unless you have a really creepy smile. Then you're in trouble.

I raised my magic wand again and said, "Ladies and gentlemen, behold!"

I stuck my hand in the box and reached into every corner. At last, I pulled out a piece of wilted lettuce covered in rabbit fur. Houdi was gone.

There was only one thing I could do. There was only one thing any magician could do. I raised the hairy lettuce into the air and held it up like it was the greatest thing on earth.

"Ta-daaaa!"

And that's when I heard the scream.

"THERE'S A RABBIT IN MY LUNCH!"

The rabbit was Houdi, of course. The screamer was Hannah Weissman. It was her job to hand out lunches at the end of class. When she opened the lunch bin, she found Houdi chewing the lettuce out of her cheese sandwich. Hannah's scream freaked Houdi out. He burrowed deeper into the lunches. A rabbit's natural instinct is to dig when frightened, and Houdi was terrified. His claws ripped into lunches as his back legs kicked like supersonic bulldozers. The food went flying. I ran to the bin and grabbed him while he thrashed and kicked. His heart beat like a snare drum as I pulled him close and tried to calm him down. I knelt in the dark closet and covered us both with my cape and whispered to him.

"It's okay, Houdi," I said. "It's okay."

He knew I was lying. It was *not* okay. The classroom went nuts with kids yelling like they'd never seen a rabbit before. Of course, somebody ran to the office to tell the principal. Somebody always has to do that. I hunkered down in the closet with Houdi and tried to cover his ears so he wouldn't hear the yelling, while Cat blocked the door. Cat is a true friend.

Eventually, Mrs. M got the class to stop yelling, but everyone kept whispering so loudly the classroom sounded like a beehive. That scared Houdi even more. How would you like to be in a buzzing beehive? Not at all.

Principal Adolphus showed up and made me put Houdi back in his box. Then he marched me and Houdi down to the office. The whole school had heard the screams from our class, so everyone was looking out their classroom doors as we went past. It's amazing how many classrooms there are on the way to the principal's office. And every one is filled with nosy kids.

Principal Adolphus made me sit in the "trouble chair" on the other side of his desk while his secretary called Mom. He leaned back in his chair and looked at me. His face was redder than usual, and a fat vein stuck out in his neck.

"Robert . . ."

"Robbie," I said.

He cleared his throat and leaned forward.

"Robbie," he said, "I'm getting reports from Mrs. Mortzchinski that you're having a hard time lately. With your grades and getting along and—"

"No, I'm not," I said.

Principal Adolphus smiled but I could tell it was a fake smile, because the vein in his neck popped out even farther.

"Are there any problems you'd like to discuss?" he said.

Like the problem my class has with rabbits? I wrapped my arms a little tighter around Houdi's box and shrugged.

He sighed.

"I see," he said. "Do you remember our conversation after last year's talent show?"

His voice told me he didn't really want an answer, so I didn't give him one.

"I specifically told you not to bring any animals to school."

"Amphibians," I said.

"What?" he asked.

"You said not to bring amphibians," I said. "Houdi is a mammal."

"I know it's a mammal," he said, and the vein in his neck stuck out even more.

"He," I said.

"What?"

"Houdi is a he," I said. "Not an it."

"Mr. Darko," he said. "I will make this very clear. Do not bring animals of any kind to this school. Do you understand?"

I shrugged. It wasn't going to be a problem. Houdi wouldn't want to come back anyway. Who would?

"I think you need to put some effort into remembering things, Robert."

Like people's names?

Principal Adolphus pointed to the bench outside the window by the flagpole.

"Your mother will pick up the rabbit in a couple of minutes."

The meeting was over. I shot out of the office and the front doors of the school and sat on the bench with the box on my lap. It felt good to get outside. I closed my eyes, lifted my face toward the sun, and took a deep breath. The warm air smelled like dirt and flowers. It was a good spring smell that made the thought of going back to class even worse. It gave me an idea.

Maybe I could go home with Mom. She wasn't big on that sort of thing. To her, leaving school required a hurricane (which is very rare in the Midwest) or life-threatening medical issues. So it was a lucky coincidence that at that moment, I developed a hacking cough . . . and a limp. There was no doubt about it. I had tuberculimpus.

Tuberculimpus is a rare and serious disease. Sometimes fatal. Always contagious. Mom would have to let me go home for the rest of the day. Maybe two days. *Cough. Cough.* Three?

Tuberculimpus is aggravated by homework and can only be cured by rest and video games. Yes, I know that going home was like running—or limping—away from my problems. But I didn't care. Facing the angry mob and Mrs. M after a weekend of gaming would be easier. It was a fifth-grade fact that I had to go back to class and catch it sooner or later, but frankly, I preferred later. Much later.

CHAPTER 13

IT WAS OBVIOUS THAT MY PLAN WAS DOOMED WHEN MOM DROVE UP WITH Grandma Melvyn in the front seat. Mom did not look happy. She jumped out of the car like a kangaroo with a jet pack. *Fast.*

"Hi . . . ," I said, and coughed. (Tuberculimpus symptom.)

Mom flung open a back passenger door and signaled for me to put Houdi's box on the seat.

"We need at least fifty-seven thousand," Mom said.

She pointed at her earpiece. Great. Mom was on the phone, which meant she would be gone in two seconds flat. I put Houdi's box on the backseat and closed the door.

A huge tuberculimpus attack rose up inside my

lungs. It was just about to come out when I looked at Grandma Melvyn. She gave me a this-is-too-funny kind of look or maybe it was a how-could-anybody-be-that-pathetic look. I couldn't tell.

"Rabbit trouble?" she asked.

And just like that, my tuberculimpus was cured. It was a miracle.

"Hold on," Mom said to the person on the phone.

She frowned at me.

"What were you thinking, Robbie?" she asked. "I don't have time for this today. Now we're late for Grandma Melvyn's doctor appointment, which makes me late for work this afternoon."

My face got hot, and my eyes started to burn. The anger drained from Mom's face and she sighed.

"Oh, kiddo," she said. "What am I going to do with you?"

Mom grabbed my shoulders to give me a hug, but I pulled away.

"Houdi needs water," I said. "Give Houdi some water."

I turned around and ran into the school without looking back.

At least one good thing came out of my speech.

Houdi destroyed so many lunches that Mrs. M ordered pizza and we had a pizza party. Everyone was happy about that except Mrs. M. Like I said, she does not like unexpected events.

The rest of the school day lasted seven years. Seven horrible, deadly, never-ending years. Cat didn't even bother trying to cheer me up at recess. Or maybe she did. It's hard to tell with Cat.

We sat beneath the ash tree by the playground. Cat braided and unbraided her hair while I dug a hole in the ground with a stick.

"Wow," she said. "That was an epic failure."

"Thanks," I said.

"No, really," she said. "It was a nuclear explosion of failure."

"Glad you liked it," I said sarcastically.

"I did!" she said. "I loved it! It was a fantastic disaster."

"Great," I said. "I created the *Hindenburg* of Rabbit Hat Tricks."

"Yep!" she said. "A great big flaming dirigible of disaster."

"Wow," I said. "I feel so much better now."

I jammed the stick hard into the ground and Cat

snatched it away from me. She poked me in the arm with it.

"Look," she said. "Accidentally having your rabbit eat everyone's lunch isn't great, but it isn't horrible. Doing it on purpose would be horrible. You didn't do it on purpose, did you?"

I gave her a look.

"Exactly," she said. "Besides, now you have a great story to tell when you're old."

Cat collects stories like other people collect T-shirts.

"Do you want to play capture the flag?" she asked.

I gave her another look. It told her exactly how much I did *not* want to do that.

"Okay," she said, handing me back my stick. "You dig a hole. I'll talk to you later. Have fun."

She didn't say it to be snotty or mean. She really meant it. Cat could actually spend the day digging holes with a stick and call it fun. She's easily amused. She's also a good friend. It takes a good friend to let you sit under a tree by yourself and poke the ground with a stick.

After about twenty minutes, the bell rang and I went back to class. There wasn't much of the day left. Only science, music, and Free Read Time.

When the final bell rang, I was out of my seat like

it was covered in hot lava. I was halfway out the door when Mrs. M called me back into the room. She made me stand there while everyone else squeezed past me.

Nate Watkins "accidentally" bumped into my shoulder on his way past.

"What's the matter, Dorko?" he whispered. "Can't make yourself disappear?"

Very funny.

When we were alone, Mrs. M got straight to the point. She tried to hide how mad she was, but it was obvious. She straightened the books on her desk, then tried to smile. She looked like she had gas.

"Robbie," she said, "I think you should resist the urge to do magic tricks in class from now on. Don't you?"

I couldn't speak. It was like someone had punched me in the gut and all my air flew out, taking my words with it. No magic? Could she do that? I could see banning rabbits maybe. Or all animals, like Principal Adolphus did. But no magic tricks at all?

I stood there trying to get my words back, but Mrs. M stood up and began stuffing her tote bag with papers. The conversation was over.

Cat was waiting for me by the flagpole to find out

what happened, but I didn't want to talk to anybody. I sneaked out the side door and cut through the vacant lot behind the school. I wanted to be alone. Cat would understand.

The field was uneven and rough. The new grass struggled to fight its way through last year's dead brown grass, but in spots, clusters of yellow dandelions and clumps of wild onions busted through.

I kicked a giant green clump, and an oniony smell rose into the air. I kicked at another clump and another. It felt good. I was about to kick a small shrub when a young brown rabbit bolted from behind it. He was barely bigger than Houdi had been when I rescued him from Mittzilla. I stopped. I had almost kicked a rabbit! How could I do that? It made me think about Houdi. I wasn't the only one who'd had a horrible day. He had been scared to death by a bunch of screaming kids and a swarm of bees, and it was all my fault. It was enough to make a rabbit give up on magic.

I picked a bunch of yellow dandelions for Houdi. He loves dandelions. I do, too. I think they're beautiful, and it makes me sad when people dig them up because they don't act like grass. They're just being themselves. Is that so bad?

I went home and took Houdi out of his cage. We sat in the Hideout and Houdi nibbled the flowers and looked at me sadly. I pulled him close and buried my face in his soft brown fur and listened to the thumping of his heart.

"I know, Houdi," I whispered. "I know."

Then something got into my eyes and made them water. It was probably just a bit of fur.

CHAPTER 14

YOU MIGHT THINK THAT THURSDAY WAS THE WORST DAY EVER. SO DID I. UNTIL Friday. Mrs. M was in a bad mood. She sat at her desk with a don't-even-think-about-it look on her face that meant business. You can say a lot of things about my classmates, but they are not stupid. They know trouble when it sits at a teacher's desk and stares them down. Nobody did anything dumb, and nobody said anything dumb. In fact, nobody said anything at all. It was spooky. At noon, Mrs. M handed out the lunches herself—just to be safe—and everyone walked silently to the lunchroom.

Remember when I said that it was a fifth-grade fact that I was going to catch it sooner or later? Well, I was right. When Mrs. M left the lunchroom, Nate pulled a small towel out of his lunch box, put it over his shoulders like a cape, and stood on the bench. Silence dropped over the room like fog at the Ice Capades. This was bad.

"Ladies and gentlemen," he said, raising a pencil into the air like a wand. "Prepare to be amazed as I pull a rabbit out of my nose!"

He paused for effect. Copycat.

"Aaahhhh . . . AAHHHHHH . . . *CHOOO!*"

Nate sneezed, and a tiny toy bunny flew out of his nose. It was one of those Teeny Beanie Bunnies from a kids' meal. The lunchroom exploded with laughter.

Hardy. Har. Har.

It didn't matter that he was lousy at sleight of hand and had obviously pulled the toy out of his pocket. It didn't matter that he used a pencil and a towel for his props. It didn't matter that he was a jerk who should be exiled to a moon base without video games for the rest of his life. None of it mattered. What mattered was that I turned red.

Bright. Tomato. Red.

I couldn't help it. I just couldn't.

"Ignore them," said Cat, but I could tell she was having a hard time not laughing, too. She stared a little too hard at her taco. Peanut butter and jelly tacos are weird, but they are *not* interesting. When Becka Scott snorted and blew a chocolate milk bubble out of her nose, even Cat lost it. She tried to hide her laughter in a fake coughing fit, but I knew what was going on.

Like I said: Hardy. Har. Har.

You want to know the scary part? That was the good part of my day!

It's shocking but true. After recess, we went back to class and I stopped making eye contact in hopes that the fake sneezing would stop. It did not. Every couple of minutes, someone let a killer sneeze fly in my direction.

Whatever.

There were only two hours until the bell and freedom. Don't get me wrong, they were two loooooooooooooooong hours, but they passed. Eventually. I lived through social studies. I lived through art. And finally, all that was left was Free Read Time. Ten glorious minutes of reading, then I was free for the whole weekend.

Just as I opened *The Life of Houdini*, Mrs. M made an announcement.

"This has been a long week," she said, looking straight at me. "So it's nice to end it with something special. Instead of our usual reading time, we're going to have another surprise visitor for Who Knew What They Do."

In case you're wondering, Who Knew What They Do is when parents come to class and talk about their jobs or hobbies or trips or whatever they want. I think it should be called Who Knew What They Do Could Be So Boring, but nobody asked me.

In case you think I'm exaggerating, I made a pie chart to show you how boring it is. I used a pie chart because the only interesting visit was when Eric's mom came to class and told us how to make pies. Those pies she brought in were delicious.

BORING VS. INTERESTING VISITS

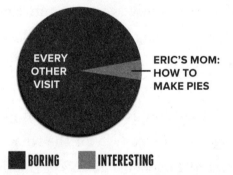

EVERY OTHER VISIT

ERIC'S MOM: HOW TO MAKE PIES

■ BORING　■ INTERESTING

Instead of reading a fascinating book about one of the world's greatest illusionists, I had to waste ten minutes listening to a surprise guest talk about raising cucumbers or grooming cats. Fine. I could sit through anything for ten minutes, because after that I was home free. I could even listen to a repeat of the most boring session of all time: Fine-Tuning Your Portfolio for High Returns. I'm looking at you, Nate Watkins's dad.

Mrs. M schedules parents to come in, but she never tells us when it will be. She thinks it's more interesting if we're surprised when they show up.

Whatever.

I put away my book, crossed my arms over my desk, and put my head down. But before I even closed my eyes, I heard something that made me sit up like a poodle at a dog biscuit factory.

"Wake up, Trixie. You might just learn something."

CHAPTER 15

GRANDMA MELVYN STOOD IN FRONT OF THE ROOM, LEANING ON HER CANE. SHE wore a glittery Niagara Falls sweatshirt and her green jogging shoes with flashing lights in the heels. She held an old cigar box under her arm. Mrs. M moved to an empty chair by the door while Grandma Melvyn set the box on Mrs. M's desk and looked around the room as if she had just landed on a weird new planet.

"Our surprise guest today is Robbie's grandmother," Mrs. M said. "She is filling in for Robbie's mom, who couldn't make it this afternoon. Let's all give Ms. Melvyn our undivided attention."

I guess that's the thing about surprise visitors. They always surprise you. Mom didn't even tell me she was supposed to come in today. She probably had some call that kept her from showing up, but it didn't matter now. The only important thing was that Grandma Melvyn was standing in front of my class with a cigar box that could contain anything. Knowing Grandma Melvyn, it wouldn't be good.

Grandma Melvyn stared at me for a second, then scanned the room.

"Here's a new word for you bunch of Trixies," she said. *"Numismatist."*

Hannah Weissman raised her hand. Grandma Melvyn gave her the Wicked Wobble Eye. Hannah Weissman lowered her hand.

"You probably think it's a lung disease," Grandma Melvyn said. "Shows what you know. A numismatist is a person who collects money."

Grandma Melvyn reached into the cigar box and pulled out a piece of blue paper with a picture of a cranky-looking man standing in front of a banner that said 5 CANADA. It looked like play money.

"This is five Canadian dollars," she said. "I got this in Niagara Falls."

She put the bill back into the box and pulled out a bill with the words 50 CANADA and a picture of an even crankier-looking man.

"I got this in Montreal," she said.

She put the bill back into the box and pulled out a plain old American ten-dollar bill.

"I got this at the gas station," she said.

Grandma Melvyn went on and on like that, pulling money out of the cigar box and saying where she got it. Some of it was crazy-colored money from other countries, and some of it was quarters she found in her couch. Grandma Melvyn never explained anything about how the money was made or why she collected it.

Surprise! Who Knew What They Do was boring. Again. But you know what? That was okay. At least Grandma Melvyn didn't make anybody cry.

I looked at the clock. Five minutes to go. I put my head down on my arms, closed my eyes, and thought about all the things I would do this weekend. I had a great list:

Not be at school.

Ride my bike.

Help Cat with her hat experiment.

Work on my sketches for a moon base prison for you know who.

I was just thinking about jet packs and robot

guards when I realized that the room was quiet. Very, *very* quiet.

I lifted my head and looked around. Grandma Melvyn was standing in front of the class with her lower lip quivering.

Wait. What had I missed?

"It's gone!" she said. "My one-dollar Canadian coin is missing."

Uh-oh.

"Maybe you dropped it on the floor," Mrs. M said, patting Grandma Melvyn's shoulder.

When had Mrs. M gotten out of her chair?

"No, I didn't!" said Grandma Melvyn. "It was right here. It's disappeared. Just like a magician made it vanish!"

WHAT?

I think the bell rang then, but I didn't hear it. I *couldn't* hear over the deafening silence of twenty-six fifth graders turning to look straight at me.

CHAPTER 16

OUTSIDE OUR ROOM, STUDENTS SWARMED THE HALL ON THEIR WAY TO freedom, but my class was trapped in a giant bubble of silence where time stood still. I saw things I hadn't noticed before: the ink spot on Mrs. M's sleeve, Hannah Weissman's shoestrings tied in a gigantic bow because they were a mile too long for her shoes, the perfectly round freckle on the side of Grandma Melvyn's chin. You notice things like that when time stands still. I would have been happy to sit there all day noticing things, but like they say: Time waits for no man.

Well, I'm here to tell you it waits for no kid either. I found that out when Mrs. M popped the time bubble with just one word.

"Robbie!"

Just like that, the spell was broken. I stood up and walked to the front of the class like a zombie.

Mrs. M glared at me. She looked like she was about to explode.

"Do you remember our conversation yesterday?"

"Yes . . . but . . . but . . ."

"That's a lot of butts for one kid," Grandma Melvyn said. "Turn out your pockets."

My zombie hands reached into my Windbreaker and pulled the pockets inside out, and as they did, four shiny silver coins spun high through the air in a glorious glittering arc. They bounced off the tile floor with a sound as sweet as shattering crystal.

Everyone gasped. And then there was that moment that doesn't have a name. It was right there staring me in the face, and I didn't even know it until the moment passed, and it passed with a vengeance. A third of the class dived under Mrs. M's desk to grab the Canadian coins. A third stood there jabbering and pointing from me to Grandma Melvyn and back again, and the other third grabbed their backpacks and ran out the door to catch their buses. A taxi pulled up to the curb outside our classroom window.

"There's my ride," said Grandma Melvyn.

She picked up her cigar box and grabbed her cane. As she started for the door, she leaned close and whispered two words that echoed in my brain and blocked out everything else. Two words that left me standing there long after Grandma Melvyn stepped into the hall and was swept away in a river of laughing, pushing students making a break for freedom . . .

"You're welcome."

CHAPTER 17

I WAITED FOR MRS. M TO LET ME HAVE IT, BUT SHE JUST SAT AT HER DESK AND shook her head.

"Go home, Robbie," she said. "Just go home."

I grabbed my backpack, ran out of the school, and sprinted toward home. I wished I had my bike, but Mom hasn't let me bike to school since a couple of bikes got stolen there. She says we can't afford to replace it if someone takes it, so I have to walk to school.

I ran all the way home. Grandma Melvyn set me up, and I wanted to know why. I was going to give her a piece of my mind. But when I got home, she wasn't there.

I found a note and a key on the kitchen table. Mom wanted me to water Grandma Melvyn's plants. Great.

I didn't feel like doing favors for Grandma Melvyn. She made me look like a thief in front of the whole class. But Mom wasn't asking; she was telling. And frankly, I was glad to get away on my bike. I pedaled so fast, the whole stinky, rotten week couldn't catch me.

It took five minutes to bike to Grandma Melvyn's house, which is a little white Monopoly house in a whole neighborhood of identical little white Monopoly houses with the same porches and the same mailboxes and the same tiny yards. You might expect Grandma Melvyn's house to have something weird about it, something that screamed "CRAZY LADY LIVES HERE." But it looked like every other house, except for the yard full of dandelions. I dropped my bike on the grass and unlocked the door.

It's not far to Grandma Melvyn's, but I hadn't been inside her house for years. When I was little, I hated going there because her couch freaked me out. It was one of those soft flowery couches you sink into when you sit down. I thought it was trying to eat me alive, and I cried every time I got near it.

Hey. I bet you were weird when you were little, too.

I stepped inside the house. The living room hadn't changed much since the last time I was there. The couch still looked hungry, and I avoided getting too close as I walked past, but you'll be glad to know that I didn't cry. The dining room table was cluttered with newspapers and a mountain of junk mail. Grandma Melvyn's house smelled like old coffee and stale news. I didn't want to linger.

I found a pitcher under the kitchen sink and watered the potted plants on the windowsill. Then I refilled the pitcher and walked down the hall to water the plants in the bathroom.

The hallway was lined with dozens of old black-and-white photographs in mismatched frames. The pictures were mismatched, too. A silver train shooting across the prairie. Men in fedoras and women in narrow skirts bustling down a skyscraper canyon. A handsome man posing in front of the Eiffel Tower. An elegant nightclub where elegant women in beaded gowns danced with men in tuxedos.

One handsome man showed up over and over again. Standing by a palm tree along a boardwalk. Walking in front of the Empire State Building. Sitting on a rock at Mount Rushmore while stone-faced presidents stared over his shoulder. I bet that was a creepy feeling.

And he wasn't the only one who showed up over

and over in the pictures. I found a woman in another picture of Mount Rushmore taken from the identical spot. She stood by the same rock, blowing a kiss to Thomas Jefferson. The woman had short, wavy hair and laughing eyes. I found a picture of her by the Eiffel Tower, too. And by that palm tree along the same boardwalk. You get the idea.

For every picture with the man, there was another with the woman. The beautiful, laughing woman with a perfectly round freckle on her chin.

Near the end of the hall, there was one missing photograph. In its place was a patch of dark blue paint with a curlicue edge where a picture frame had hidden the wall for so long that everything around it had faded to a soft, sad blue while the paint behind it stayed dark. The picture was gone, but the dark blue patch lingered like a memory. A ghost. What was the missing picture?

I finished watering the plants, locked the house, and biked home.

CHAPTER 18

I HAD AVOIDED GRANDMA MELVYN SINCE SHE MOVED IN, AND I GUESS IT WAS bugging Mom, because on Saturday night she made me sit by Grandma Melvyn at dinner. We ate in the dining room. I hadn't been there since Mom's party, and going back felt like returning to the scene of the crime. I couldn't wait for dinner to end.

Grandma Melvyn didn't say anything while she ate, but she never took her eyes off me. I tried to stare back at her, but it was like having a staring contest with an owl. Not a winning situation.

After dinner, Mom and Ape Boy did the dishes. Ape Boy loves putting the dishes away because it involves climbing on chairs and countertops when Mom's not looking. Grandma Melvyn and I sat at the table with our bowls of ice cream. She poked me with her cane.

"Are you going to thank me?" she asked. "That coin trick was pretty good."

"What are you talking about?" I said. "Everyone thinks I'm a thief!"

"Correction," said Grandma Melvyn. "Everyone thinks you're a clever thief. Big difference. At least they're thinking about you. You can't buy that kind of press."

"Wha . . . Why . . . Wha . . . ?"

"Don't fry your brain over it," she said. "I stuck the coins in your pocket the night before, when your teacher called to remind your mom to come to class. Trixie looked so frazzled, I decided to go instead."

"Why?"

"Somebody needs to help you with your act."

"What are you talking about?" I asked suspiciously.

"I'm going to help you with your magic act," she said. "Though you could use some fashion help, too. Did your mother buy that shirt for you?"

"I'm eleven," I said.

"It shows," she said.

I thought about making a crack about her tacky

sweatshirts and her sparkly shoes, but I didn't. I want to live to see sixth grade.

"What do you know about my act?" I asked.

"Enough to know you need help," she said. "If I'm stuck in Trixieville, I might as well have a hobby. You're as good as the next. Let's start with a disappearing act."

Grandma Melvyn ate the rest of her ice cream and licked the spoon.

"Ta-daaaa!"

She snorted and stood up.

"Classic," she said. "Oh yeah, it arrived today. Trixie made them put it in the garage. Some people have no clue."

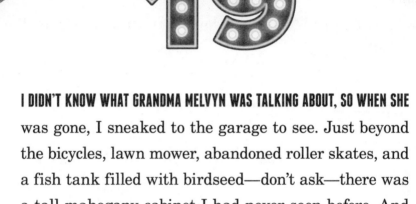

CHAPTER 19

I DIDN'T KNOW WHAT GRANDMA MELVYN WAS TALKING ABOUT, SO WHEN SHE was gone, I sneaked to the garage to see. Just beyond the bicycles, lawn mower, abandoned roller skates, and a fish tank filled with birdseed—don't ask—there was a tall mahogany cabinet I had never seen before. And it wasn't any old cabinet. I had seen cabinets like it in catalogs for magicians. My heart beat faster as I looked closer. It was beautiful. It was at least six feet tall and four feet wide with four small wheels at the base. I twirled it around and looked at each side. They were identical. No doors. No handles. No obvious way to open it. I got on the floor and felt under the cabinet for a latch. The bottom was solid wood.

I twirled the cabinet very slowly, examining each

panel. On the third side, I found an unusual spot in the grain about two feet above the floor. The grain of the wood in one spot whorled tightly, like a thumbprint. I pushed on it and the panel creaked open, revealing the black velvet interior of a magician's disappearing cabinet.

I heard a noise behind me and turned around. Grandma Melvyn was standing in the doorway.

"Magic lessons start tomorrow," she said.

Then Grandma Melvyn turned and disappeared into the house. Maybe it was my imagination, but I think she was just a little bit taller than before.

CHAPTER 20

MAGIC LESSONS START TOMORROW.

I couldn't sleep just thinking about it. Actually, I couldn't sleep for three reasons:

1. There was a real magician's cabinet in the garage, and it belonged to Grandma Melvyn. What did she know about magic?

2. Grandma Melvyn wanted to give me "magic lessons"? I didn't have a clue what that meant. It might be good, or it might be very *not* good. Correction, make that extremely, very, very not good.

3. Ape Boy found Mom's stash of dark chocolate and ate it all. He spent the night swinging onto the top bunk and jumping off again. Each time I got to sleep, he peeked into the Hideout and whispered,

"Are you asleep? I'm not asleep. Are you asleep? How come you're not asleep? Want some gum? Yay!"

Ape Boy settled down at four in the morning, but by then I was wide awake. I couldn't stop thinking about the cabinet. Then I got an idea.

Maybe—and it was an elephant-sized maybe—I could use the cabinet in the talent show. After all, Grandma Melvyn had humiliated me in front of the entire class, even if she didn't think so. Letting me use the cabinet would make up for that . . . a little.

If I had a real magician's cabinet, I would have the greatest act ever. At least the greatest act in the history of the Hobson Elementary School Talent Show. Yes, I know that's a very low standard. Thank you very much for pointing that out. But every magician has to start somewhere.

With Grandma Melvyn's cabinet, I could show everyone that I was a real magician. For once, I could stand on the stage in front of the whole world, and when that moment with no name arrived, everyone would know what came next. No screams. No fire trucks. Just me taking the biggest bow of my life to thunderous applause and cheers: *Bravo! Encore! Well done, kiddo.* There couldn't be a better way to end my career at Hobson than that!

It was almost dawn when I finally drifted to sleep, and I'm pretty sure I was smiling when I did.

When my alarm went off, I wanted to keep sleeping. I had a feeling that I'd dreamed up the whole thing—including the cabinet. Eventually, I dragged myself to the kitchen. Grandma Melvyn was sitting at the table, drinking coffee. I walked past her and opened the door into the garage from the family room. I smiled and closed the door. It was there.

The cabinet was real, and I was going to find a way to get Grandma Melvyn to let me use it in the talent show. I would start by being nice to her. Super nice. I went back to the kitchen and smiled at Grandma Melvyn.

"Do you have gas?" she asked.

I smiled harder.

"Are you going to puke?" she asked.

I stopped smiling and went to plan B: conversation.

"How are you?" I asked.

"Who wants to know?"

Okay, plan C: awkward silence.

Grandma Melvyn looked at me. I looked at the floor.

Grandma Melvyn looked at me again. I looked at the refrigerator. I looked at my fingers. I looked at my shoes. You get the idea.

At last, she coughed, and I looked at *her*.

"So you want to learn magic?" she asked.

"Yes," I said.

"Well, there's no such thing as magic. Now go back to bed. I've seen mummies who looked more awake than you."

So much for magic lessons.

CHAPTER 21

I MARCHED BACK TO THE HIDEOUT AND WENT TO SLEEP. WHEN I WOKE UP I WAS hungry, so I went back to the kitchen. Mom was shopping with Ape Boy—probably for ape chow—and Grandma Melvyn was by the sink. Great.

I fixed myself a bowl of cereal and sat down. There was a five-dollar bill on the table.

"Trixie left your allowance," Grandma Melvyn said.

I reached for the money, but before I could grab it, Grandma Melvyn set a clear glass of water right on top of it.

"Pick that up," she said, as if I'd put it down on the money in the first place.

I picked up the glass as she put a green tablet in the water. It fizzed and bubbled. Then she reached into her mouth, pulled out a tooth, and plopped it into the fizzy green water. I almost dropped the glass.

"News flash," she said. "You'd make a lousy Tooth Fairy, too. Better study hard in school. Your career options are dwindling."

A storm of tiny scrubbing bubbles engulfed the tooth as it sank to the bottom of the glass.

"Ewww," I said.

"Don't have a seizure," she said. "It's a ceramic tooth. Put down the glass."

I swept the money off the table with my free hand and stuffed it into my pocket. Then I set the glass on the table. Grandma Melvyn walked to the doorway and turned around.

"It's a funny thing," she said. "The closer you look, the less you see. You were so busy freaking out about a fake tooth that you wouldn't have noticed if an elephant marched in and dropped a load on your shoes."

She limped down the hall, then yelled back at me.

"Keep the change."

"*Wha . . . ?*"

I pulled the crumpled money from my pocket, smoothed it on the table, and frowned while Mr. George Washington, first president of the United States of America, smiled back at me.

CHAPTER 22

MY CHEEKS BURNED AS IF GRANDMA MELVYN HAD THROWN THE BIGGEST Beanie Bunny of them all and hit me smack in the face. She had just swapped my five dollars for a lousy one-dollar bill. In other words, she had stolen four dollars from me, but that wasn't the worst part. She'd held out magic lessons like a lollipop to a little kid and then just jerked them away. What had I been thinking, trusting her in the first place? Just like Nate Watkins said, I was a dork.

I sat at the table and got madder and madder. Finally, I marched into the family room. Grandma Melvyn sat in the recliner watching *Wheel of Fortune*. In case you have a real life and have missed it, *Wheel of Fortune* is a TV game show where an audience watches people play hangman with prizes. It's weird. I always thought watching it was boring, but I guess I wasn't doing it right, because Grandma Melvyn was having a blast.

"Buy a vowel, Trixie!" she yelled at a middle-aged man in a golf shirt.

"Forget the z!" she snapped at a red-headed woman. "This isn't Czechoslovakia!"

I stood there trying to say one of the million thoughts crashing around in my head, but all that came out was "I . . . I . . . I . . ."

"You've got more eyes than a spider," Grandma Melvyn said without looking at me. "If you want something, spit it out."

I grabbed one of the million thoughts and spit it out.

"Give me my money," I said.

Grandma Melvyn laughed.

"Why should I?" she asked.

"Because it's mine," I said.

Grandma Melvyn flipped off the television and gave me the Wicked Wobble Eye.

I stared right back at her.

"People take things that don't belong to them all

the time," said Grandma Melvyn. "Why should I be any different?"

"Because you are," I said.

That was *not* what I was going to say, and the words shocked me almost as much as they shocked Grandma Melvyn.

"You don't know anything about me," she said.

Grandma Melvyn cleared her throat and narrowed her eyes as she stared at me. For once, her eyes did not wobble behind her thick glasses. They were still and clear, and they cut right into me.

"The fiver pays for lessons," she said. "If that's the only price you pay for magic, you're lucky."

Grandma Melvyn flipped on the television just as the audience cheered for a blond woman who grabbed the enormous wheel and sent it whirling.

"You spin like a two-year-old!" Grandma Melvyn yelled.

The conversation was over. As I left the family room, the million thoughts crashing around in my mind were replaced by only one thing: the price of magic.

I didn't know what that meant, but I had the feeling that for Grandma Melvyn, it had nothing to do with money.

CHAPTER 23

THE CONVERSATION LEFT ME MORE CONFUSED THAN EVER. WAS GRANDMA Melvyn just teasing me, or was she actually going to teach me some magic? And what did she know about magic, anyway? What *could* she know? Probably nothing. But if that was true, why did she have that cabinet? That amazing, perfect magician's cabinet? It was not a fake-o cabinet like my fake-o cape. That cabinet was the real deal.

I didn't know the answers to any of these questions, but I decided to get them. And I decided something else, too. If Grandma Melvyn wanted to play tough, so could I. If I was paying for magic lessons, I was getting magic lessons. End of story.

When I got home from school the next day, Grandma

Melvyn was at the kitchen table. I sat down next to her and didn't say a word.

"Got a problem?" she asked.

"Nope," I said. "Just waiting for my lesson."

"Here's a lesson. Never eat chili before bed."

I glared at her.

"Here's another lesson," she said. "Don't waste your time with whiners or wannabes."

She got up and went to the family room. She was leaning harder on her cane than usual, and when she sat in the recliner, she gasped softly as she lifted her leg onto the footrest. Her knee hurt. Or maybe . . .

Maybe Grandma Melvyn was faking it.

She reached for the zapper, but I snatched it first and plopped onto the couch, and before you say anything—yeah, I know. Stealing a zapper from an old lady with a bad knee isn't cool, but it was Grandma Melvyn and she was only faking . . . and . . . Oh, be quiet. I know it wasn't my finest moment, but I meant business.

Grandma Melvyn leaned back in the recliner and gave me the Wicked Wobble Eye as expected. I glared back at her. The time was 3:30 P.M. I was prepared to sit there glaring at Grandma Melvyn for as long as it took for her to keep her end of the deal and teach me some magic. (If she actually knew any.)

3:31.

3:32.

3:33.

3:40.

3:47. The doorbell rang. I ignored it.

4:07.

4:08. Mom and Ape Boy came home. I ignored them.

4:11.

4:13. Ape Boy climbed onto the back of the couch and blew a gigantic bubble three inches from my ear. I popped it without taking my eyes off Grandma Melvyn. Ape Boy ran off screaming.

4:17. Grandma Melvyn pulled a pair of clippers from her pocket and clipped her toenails without taking her eyes off me. I wanted to run off screaming.

4:28. I tried not to think about the six gallons of water I drank after running laps in gym class.

4:29. I crossed my legs.

4:29:01. I tried not to think about rivers, streams, creeks, or any other form of running water.

4:29:03. I tried not to think of lakes, ponds, puddles, ice cubes, or any other form of not-running water.

4:29:06. I uncrossed my legs and recrossed them.

4:29:08. Grandma Melvyn's eyes narrowed behind her thick glasses and she smiled slyly.

4:29:10. She drummed her fingers on the arm of the recliner and sang, "'Raindrops keep fallin' on my head'..."

4:29:25. I tried not to think about raindrops.

4:29:26. I tried not to think about water fountains. Water slides. Water bottles. Water parks.

4:29:27. Trying not to think about water parks reminded me of swimming pools. Swimming holes. Swimming whales spewing water into the air in a watery fountain of watery water.

4:29:31. Grandma Melvyn said, "Do you know what I love, Robbie? I love waterfalls. Big splashy, splashy waterfalls with all that splashing wet water that splashes around. Don't you?"

4:29:32. Grandma Melvyn imitated the sound of a waterfall. I did *not* love it.

4:29:33. I thought about the Gobi Desert. The Mohave Desert. Desert islands . . . which are basically small deserts . . . surrounded by . . . Yep, you guessed it. Water.

4:29:35. Grandma Melvyn said, "You know what

else I love, Robbie? I love the sound of a leaky faucet. Don't you?"

4:29:36. I sighed.

4:29:37. Grandma Melvyn smiled.

4:29:38. "Drip . . . Drip . . . Dri—"

4:29:38:01. I ran to the bathroom as Grandma Melvyn yelled after me, "Never start anything you can't finish."

CHAPTER 24

THE NEXT DAY, I SKIPPED THE DRINKING FOUNTAIN AFTER GYM AND MADE A pit stop before I left school—if you know what I mean, and I think you do. This time, I was absolutely ready to march into the house, sit right down, and stare at Grandma Melvyn for as long as it took for her to live up to her part of the bargain. But when I got home, the garage door was open and Grandma Melvyn was sitting inside on a lawn chair next to the mahogany box.

"Took you long enough," she said. "A person could die from birdseed poisoning in this junk shop you call a garage."

She pointed at the magician's box.

"Figure it out," she said.

"Wait," I said suspiciously. "Are you *really* going to teach me something?"

"What do you think I've been doing?" she asked.

"Taking my money," I said.

"Shows what you know," she said, pointing toward the cabinet again. "I'm not getting any younger."

I dropped my backpack and twirled the cabinet until I found the twisted knot on the mahogany panel. I pushed on the knot, and the panel opened with a slow creaking sound. I wanted to say "Ha!" but I just smiled. She did not. She was not impressed.

"You want a Nobel Prize?" she asked.

"No . . . I just . . ."

"Well," she said, "what's next?"

"I get inside?" I said, only half sure that was the right answer.

Grandma Melvyn shrugged.

I stepped inside the magician's cabinet. It smelled like a stale closet no one had touched in a century. I ran my hand over the smooth black velvet walls. The trampled velvet on the floor shimmered in the light.

"Shut the door," I said.

"If you say so," she said.

Grandma Melvyn pushed the panel shut with her

cane. I expected the inside of the cabinet to be totally dark, but slivers of light streamed in from the oval-shaped holes running up and down the sides of the cabinet. More light came through the soda-can-size holes in the ceiling. The holes would be invisible to the audience, but they would let in air and enough light for the assistant to see during the trick. That was a smart design.

I hadn't noticed the ceiling holes the other night, but it was dark in the garage then and I hadn't looked up. Not looking up was the kind of thing a moron in a horror movie would do—or not do. Have you ever noticed that? If people in horror movies ever looked up, they'd see half the things that are about to kill them and they'd just run away. I made a note to myself to look up more often.

Even with the holes in the top, the cabinet was stuffy, so I got busy trying to get out. I ran my hands along the velvet walls searching for a mechanism to reopen the panel. No luck. I pushed on two sides at once. Then the other two sides. I stamped on the floor. I poked my finger into each of the tiny holes in the sides hoping to flip a trigger or something. Nothing. Then I had a thought. A very important thought. A thought I wish I had considered before I asked Grandma Melvyn to shut the panel. Maybe the trick required an assistant to open it from the outside.

Oh.

I could just hear Grandma Melvyn busting a gut outside the locked cabinet. Wait a minute. No, I couldn't. I pressed my ear against the velvet wall and listened. I couldn't hear anything. I peeked out one of the holes on the cabinet's sides, but I couldn't see her.

"Grandma Melvyn?" I said.

Silence.

"Hello?" I said louder.

Silence.

"HELLOOOO?"

Deafening silence.

My face burned, but this time it wasn't from anger. It was embarrassment. Grandma Melvyn was testing me, and I'd failed. A real magician should think before acting. Magic is about the brain, and a magician who doesn't use his brain is just a wannabe. I deserved to be stuck inside the cabinet. I should have known what was going to happen before I ever asked her to close the door in the first place.

The floor was big enough for me to sit cross-legged,

so I sat down to wait until Mom sent out a search party for me or I starved to death—whichever came first.

After a few minutes, the panel swung open. Grandma Melvyn leaned on her cane and looked down at me sitting on the crushed-velvet floor. She didn't say a word, and neither did I. After all, what could I say?

Grandma Melvyn sat down on the lawn chair, and I climbed out of the cabinet. She tapped her cane impatiently on the concrete garage floor.

"Here's the deal, Mr. Robbie Darko," she said. "I don't waste my time on lazy people. There are no shortcuts. If you want *my* time, pay attention."

She pulled a quarter out of thin air, held it out to me, then pulled it back.

"And if you cry like you did at your fifth birthday party," she said, "we're done."

"Did you give me the coin trick at my party?" I asked.

"What do you think, Einstein?" she said. "Do you know anyone else with a clue?"

She tossed me the quarter.

"Impress me," she said.

I rolled the quarter over my knuckles in one direction and then back again, and then flipped it into my palm, closed my fist around it, and blew a puff of air onto my fist. When I opened my hand, the quarter was gone. (Remember how I said I used to practice coin tricks in class? I wasn't kidding.)

"Whoop-dee-doo," Grandma Melvyn said. "You just alerted the audience to the fact that you can handle a coin. Now when it appears somewhere, they'll know you used skill to do it and not magic."

"But people like fancy finger work," I said.

"So what," said Grandma Melvyn. "People like triple cheeseburgers with double bacon. Doesn't mean you have to give it to them. Your job is to make them believe impossible things. If they know you can handle a coin, the impossible becomes possible. Skill kills magic. Showing off is for jugglers. Got it?"

"Got it," I said.

"I doubt it," she said.

She pulled a second quarter out of thin air and handed it to me.

"Now show me what you can do with your left hand," she said.

"But wouldn't that be showing off my skill?" I asked.

"It would be if you had any," she said.

"But you just said—"

Grandma Melvyn gave me the Wicked Wobble Eye. I put the first quarter onto my left knuckle and rolled it back and forth almost as smoothly as I had done with my right hand. I grinned ear to ear.

"Now do both," Grandma Melvyn said.

Easy.

"In opposite directions," she said.

Oh.

I put the first quarter on my right knuckles like before. I put the second quarter on my left knuckles and started. The quarters flew into the air and bounced off the concrete floor into a heap of junk by the birdseed aquarium.

"Impressive," said Grandma Melvyn, as she opened the door to the family room.

I spent the next two hours practicing and hunting for the quarters. Well, mostly hunting for quarters. While I dug through the garage junk, I thought about Grandma Melvyn and my birthday presents. She had given me the coin trick. She must have given me the top hat on my ninth birthday, too.

Who *was* Grandma Melvyn?

CHAPTER 25

THE NEXT DAY OF MAGIC LESSONS WAS PRETTY MUCH THE SAME, EXCEPT THAT Grandma Melvyn sat in the recliner in the family room watching another *Wheel of Fortune* marathon while I worked on quarter rolling in the garage. I could hear her yelling at the TV through the door that led from the garage to the family room. All I can say is that it's a good thing Grandma Melvyn was watching from home instead of the studio audience. Who knew game shows could be so violent?

Rolling quarters over my knuckles was not exciting, and doing it for hours made my hands sore. But it helped. The second day, I only spent one-third of my time hunting for quarters in the junk pile. The next day, only a fourth. After each day of practice, I improved. Maybe someday I could roll quarters without digging through junk at all. It seemed like I would be rolling quarters forever, but one day, when I got home from school, Grandma Melvyn was sitting at the kitchen table with a deck of cards.

"It's time for a joker sandwich," she said.

"What's that?" I asked.

She answered with the Wicked Wobble Eye, which, it turns out, is her favorite answer to almost every question. I stopped talking and sat in the chair next to her. Grandma Melvyn pulled two jokers out of the deck and laid them faceup on the table. Then she shuffled the deck and held it out to me.

"Cut the deck and take the top card," she said.

I lifted the top half of the deck and picked the seven of clubs from the bottom pile of cards. Grandma Melvyn nodded for me to stick my card back in the deck, so I did. After that, Grandma Melvyn put the jokers back in the deck and shuffled it. Then she coughed. (I'm not sure if the cough was important, but with Grandma Melvyn anything is possible. In any case, it was a big cough.)

Finally, Grandma Melvyn pulled three cards off the top of the deck and held them out to me.

"Here's your sandwich," she said.

I took the cards and looked at them. They were the two jokers on the outside, like slices of bread, with my seven of clubs squished in between like a slice of bologna.

"How did you do that?" I asked.

Wicked Wobble Eye. (See what I mean about that being the answer to everything?)

"That's the joker sandwich," she said. "Now let's do a tomato-cheese sandwich."

"How does it work?" I asked.

"You get up and make one," she said.

"That's funny," I said.

"Why is that funny?" she asked, looking at me suspiciously. "Is the cheese moldy?"

"Wait," I said. "You really want me to make you a sandwich?"

"They don't make themselves," Grandma Melvyn said.

Again . . . Wicked Wobble Eye.

I am not a great cook, but I got up to make Grandma Melvyn a cheese-and-tomato sandwich. While I looked for a knife, Grandma Melvyn picked up the cards and began to shuffle. Her hands were a blur as she shuffled over and over, each time moving the cards in a new shuffle. She knew more ways to shuffle cards than I had ever seen. Grandma Melvyn spread the cards into a single fan, then two fans. Then four fans. She waved the fans, and they melted into a single square deck, which she instantly stretched into a long card bridge. With a flick of her thumb, the cards gracefully flipped over one by one, cascading like a run of dominoes. She swept the cards together, shuffled once more, and swept them into a perfect fan arranged by suit: Spades, then hearts. Clubs, then diamonds.

Grandma Melvyn was showing off exactly like she'd told me not to do. And in case you were wondering, I did not point it out to her. I'm not an idiot. Besides, I was having too much fun watching her in action. I cut one thick slice of tomato (and almost one thick slice of my finger because I was too busy watching Grandma Melvyn to pay attention to making the sandwich), then I stuffed the tomato and a slice of cheese between two pieces of bread, tossed the sandwich onto a saucer, and sat down at the table.

As I sat down, Grandma Melvyn set the cards on the table and scooted them toward me. She took a bite of her sandwich and nodded toward the cards. The show was over. It was my turn.

I used to think that my shuffling was impressive, and maybe it is—for a fifth grader. But after watching Grandma Melvyn at work, I felt like my hands were gigantic blobs of rubber that I had no control over. I fumbled my shuffle, and half the cards fell on the floor.

"Sorry," I said.

Grandma Melvyn raised an eyebrow and took another bite of her sandwich. I picked up the cards, squared them into a neat deck, took a deep breath, and began again. The cards slipped together in a clean shuffle. I did it again, then again, faster with each shuffle. Each time, I squared the deck perfectly before splitting it into two halves. Real card experts know exactly how many cards are in a stack just by the thickness of the stack. They do almost everything by feel. That is very important for tricks where you need to know the exact position of a card. I squeezed each half of the deck tightly, trying to tell if they had the same number of cards.

"Are you trying to squeeze the ink off those cards?" Grandma Melvyn asked.

I loosened my grip.

"The audience might be a bunch of Trixies," Grandma Melvyn said, "but they can tell when you're tense, and it makes them tense, too. It makes them pay close attention, and then it's all over."

I loosened my grip again and shuffled while Grandma Melvyn ate the last bite of her sandwich. The shuffle was smoother.

"Not bad," Grandma Melvyn said, standing up and heading for the family room.

I smiled.

"But next time, add mayo."

CHAPTER 26

WHEN I CAME HOME THE NEXT DAY, GRANDMA MELVYN WAS SLEEPING IN THE recliner beneath a crocheted afghan. I sat on the couch and stared at her, hoping she would wake up so we could work on something, but she snored away. I thought about shaking her arm or running around the room yelling "Zoysia attack!" but I didn't know what would happen if I woke Grandma Melvyn. It had the potential to be dangerous—like when a startled sleepwalker goes crazy and murders some stranger on the sidewalk. I went to the kitchen table and pulled a pack of cards out of my backpack and practiced shuffling.

I split the deck into different-sized stacks and counted the cards in each stack. Then I closed my eyes and picked up each one without "squeezing the ink off it." I concentrated on the thickness of each stack and how it felt in my hands. I tried to imprint the feel of each stack in my mind so I could remember it later. Twenty-seven cards feel like this. Fifteen cards feel like that. After a while, I reversed the process and tried to guess how many cards were in a stack just by feel. I was never right, but sometimes I was close. Once, I was just twelve off. Okay, so that's not impressive, since there are only fifty-two cards to start with. I needed lots more practice.

I shuffled and reshuffled and reshuffled the cards. When I was done with that, I shuffled and reshuffled and reshuffled them all over again. And you know what? It was fun. I was focused like a laser and lost track of time until—*cough!*

I jumped out of the chair and turned around. Grandma Melvyn was standing there watching me shuffle. I don't know how long she'd been there, but it might have been a long time. I looked at the clock. I'd been shuffling for almost two hours.

Without a word, Grandma Melvyn smiled slightly, nodded her head at me, and went back to the recliner. And you know what? Even though we had already been working together for almost a week, that was the moment when my magic lessons really started. I don't mean that anything changed about what we did in lessons. The lessons were still weird, and I never knew what was going to happen. What was different was Grandma Melvyn. Before that moment, she didn't seem to care if I got anything out of lessons or not.

After that moment, she got serious.

CHAPTER 27

FRIDAY NIGHT, I HELPED MOM SET THE TABLE FOR DINNER.

"I never thanked you for the tablecloth trick," she said.

"It didn't turn out right."

"I know," she said. "But you worked on it a long time. Thank you."

I smiled.

"Hey, kiddo," she said. "After I get Harry to bed, do you want to pick out a movie?"

"Yeah!" I said. "I'll make the popcorn and you get the candy."

I thought about movies all through dinner. I couldn't decide between *Top Hat*, which is Mom's all-time favorite Fred Astaire movie, or *Casablanca*, which is my all-time favorite old movie. It doesn't have any dancing, but it has lots of suspense. In the end, I decided to let Mom pick. Of course she would pick *Top Hat*, and that was okay. I like Fred Astaire. He was like a dancing magician. He never left anything to chance. He practiced and practiced until his act was perfect.

By nine o'clock, Ape Boy and Grandma Melvyn were both out of the family room. Ape Boy was in bed and Grandma Melvyn was in my old room. Mom sat on the couch with the box of Reese's Pieces and the movies. While she decided which one to watch, I went to the kitchen and put a bag of popcorn into the microwave. Two minutes and forty seconds later, it was movie time!

I opened the steaming bag of popcorn, poured it into the big silver popcorn bowl, and went to the family room.

"Did you pick *Top Hat* or *Casabla—*"

Mom was fast asleep; the movies and box of candy lay on the floor beside the couch. So much for Movie Night.

I went back to the kitchen and sat at the table. I picked a piece of popcorn out of the bowl and threw it at the trash can. I missed. I tossed another and another. I missed.

"Your aim is almost as bad as your bow."

Grandma Melvyn was standing in the doorway.

"If you're going to waste popcorn," she said, "you should do it right."

She sat down beside me and picked up a piece of popcorn and tossed it right into the basket.

"Two points," she said. "Your problem is weak hands."

"I don't have weak hands," I said.

Grandma Melvyn reached her hand out to me with her thumb up and her fingers bent at the knuckles.

"Wrestle," she said.

"Huh?"

"Put your puny little baby thumb here, and thumb wrestle," she said.

"I don't have a puny baby thumb," I said.

"That's what all the puny babies say," said Grandma Melvyn. "Count."

I locked my fingertips into hers in the classic thumb-wrestling position. Her fingers were bony and cool. I wagged my thumb back and forth and started counting.

"One. Two. Three. Four. I declare a thumb war. Five. Six. Hey!"

Grandma Melvyn pinned my thumb. I tried to pull it free, but her grip was like iron.

"Hey!" I said. "You have to wait until I say 'Five. Six. Seven. Eight. Try to keep your thumb—'"

She pinned my thumb again.

"I wasn't ready," I said.

"Oh, I'm sorry," she said in a way that meant exactly the opposite. She released my thumb and I started again.

"One. Two. Hey!"

She pinned my thumb a third time. And it hurt.

"Both thumbs," she said, releasing my thumb and extending her left hand.

I want to say that what followed was a thumb-wrestling championship in which I was crowned the greatest thumb wrestler of all time. That would be a lie. What actually happened was a thumb-wrestling massacre. No matter how I moved to dodge her attack or pin her thumbs, Grandma Melvyn was faster. Her bony thumbs were fast, furious, and ferocious. The massacre lasted all of one minute before Grandma Melvyn let go of my hands.

"Puny baby thumbs," she said.

I knew when I was defeated.

"So what," I said.

"So," she said. "You'll never master cards, coins, or anything with puny baby thumbs. I can fix that."

Grandma Melvyn spent the next hour showing me finger exercises. Most people have one hand that is much stronger than the other. And even on that hand, some fingers are strong and some are weak. (I'm looking at you, Ring Finger and Pinky.) That's fine for most people. But not for magicians. A magician needs to hold coins and cards and all sorts of things without anyone seeing what they are doing. Every finger must be able to work independently. It sounds easy, but it's really hard.

Grandma Melvyn showed me how to lock my fingers together and then move them in patterns to build the muscles in each finger. If I practice every night and every morning and every science class and every English class and . . . you get the idea . . . my shuffles would get smoother and my sleight of hand would be better.

Finally, Grandma Melvyn stood up and walked out of the kitchen.

"Keep practicing, and your puny baby fingers will grow up nice and strong," she said. "Then we'll work on the puny baby bow of yours."

I threw away the popcorn that had fallen on the floor and went to the family room, where Mom was still asleep on the couch with the movies and candy on the floor beside her. I gently covered her with the crocheted afghan, flipped off the light, and went upstairs to bed.

CHAPTER 28

HAVE YOU EVER SEEN A MOVIE WHERE A CHARACTER WANTS TO WIN SOME KIND of competition and someone helps them learn everything they need to know and weeks pass by in only three movie minutes? The whole time you watch, an inspirational song plays, and in the end, the character wins the muskrat rodeo/cheese-eating contest/platypus-throwing tournament or whatever they are trying to win and everyone lives happily ever after. If you've never seen this, you ought to get out more, because it happens in *every* movie I watch. They call it a montage. The last part of the word sounds like the end of the word *garage*, in case you're wondering how to pronounce it.

Montages are movie tricks to get past the boring stuff and on to the good stuff. It's kind of like watching a couple seconds of basketball practice every day for a week so you can see how hard the team works to get ready for the big game.

I want to get to the exciting part of my story—hint, it's the talent show—but first I need to tell you more about Grandma Melvyn's magic lessons.

I could write about everything we did, but I'd need a thousand pages and that could take all afternoon. Plus, it might reveal some magic secrets, and you already know I'm not going to do that. So I'm going to do something that has never been tried before in a book. I'm going to do a montage!

Instead of describing every magic lesson to you, I'll condense them into a few short seconds. But I need your help.

The most important part of any montage is the music. For this to work, you have to sing along while you read. A catchy and inspirational song is best. I can't hear what you're singing, so I'm going to trust you to pick a great song. Here's a hint. Do *not* use the songs in the following chart. (And in case you're wondering, they are real songs. Look them up if you don't believe me.)

Oh yeah, there's one more song you can*not* use: "Raindrops Keep Fallin' on My Head." You know why.

DO *NOT* USE THESE SONGS!

1. "You're the Reason Our Kids Are So Ugly"
2. "I've Been Flushed from the Bathroom of Your Heart"
3. "I Would Have Wrote You a Letter, but I Couldn't Spell Yuck!"
4. "They May Put Me in Prison, but They Can't Stop My Face from Breakin' Out"
5. "Mama, Get the Hammer (There's a Fly on Papa's Head)"
6. "Her Teeth Were Stained, but Her Heart Was Pure"
7. "If My Nose Were Full of Nickels, I'd Blow It All on You"

Okay. Here's the montage of Grandma Melvyn's magic lessons. It starts with Grandma Melvyn and me at the kitchen table. She's teaching me a new shuffle.

Okay. Get ready to sing . . .

Aaaaaaannnnnndddddd ACTION!

. . . You call that a shuffle? . . . *I got it! I got it!* . . . *Oops* . . . That stunk . . . *I'll pick them up* . . . I've seen golf clubs with better grips . . . *Oops* . . . Call me when you find them . . . *Thirty-one, thirty-two* . . . Start over! . . . *Oops!* . . . *Sixteen, seventeen* . . . Buy a vowel, Trixie!

. . . Copy what I'm doing . . . *Like that?* . . . Exactly *not* like that . . . *But, how* . . . The eye sees only what the mind is prepared to see . . . *I see* . . . No, I don't . . . Exactly . . . *Wait . . . what?* . . .

. . . Watch my right hand . . . *How did you* . . . With my left hand . . . *But you said* . . . Which is more important, what I do or what I say? . . . *Ohhhhhh! I got it!* . . . Yes, you do. Take a bow . . . *Oops!* . . . Get the fire extinguisher.

Aaaaaaannnnnndddddd CUT!

I left out a lot of stuff, including the bit where I got my hand stuck in a pickle jar and the bit where I got my ankle tied to the birdcage and the bit where . . . Never mind. You get the idea.

The point is that Grandma Melvyn and I worked every day after school, and I spent hours and hours and hours (and hours and hours and hours) shuffling cards and palming coins and passing things from one hand to the other over and over again. I also spent a lot of time playing fifty-two-card pickup, which is where you pick up fifty-two cards after you drop them. Fun, right?

But you know what? It was fun. And even when it wasn't fun, it was important. All that stuff is called small magic. And it's a big part of most magic acts. If you can pull off small magic, the audience will trust you on the big magic. At least that's how it's supposed to work. You'll just have to keep reading to see if it really does.

Do you like the way I added a teaser there? That's part of a good magic act, too. Keep them guessing what happens next.

CHAPTER 29

AFTER ALMOST TWO WEEKS OF MAGIC LESSONS, I DECIDED IT WAS TIME TO make my move and ask Grandma Melvyn if I could use the cabinet in the talent show. She crossed her arms over her rhinestone-bedazzled VIVA LAS VEGAS sweatshirt and looked at me suspiciously.

"Why should I?" she asked.

"Because it would give the Trixies down at the booger mines something to talk about," I said.

She thought about it for a second.

"Good reason," she said.

If Grandma Melvyn hadn't been sitting in the lawn chair—and armed with a cane—I would have hugged her! Well, maybe I would have shaken her hand vigorously—except she'd probably crush my hand with her grip of steel. Okay, I'd say thank you and smile like an idiot. Which is exactly what I did.

"Don't count your chickens before your final bow," she said. "Which, as I recall, stinks."

She unfolded her arms and smiled in a way I hadn't seen before, and for the first time, I saw a twinkle in her eye and just a hint of the young woman from the photos.

"You'll need an assistant," Grandma Melvyn said.

"Cat can do it!" I said. "She's awesome. You're going to love her!"

And just like that, the twinkle in Grandma Melvyn's eye flickered out. Her smile vanished, and with it, the echo of the young woman in the photo. Grandma Melvyn leaned onto her cane and got out of the lawn chair.

"Some things never change," she said.

CHAPTER 30

GRANDMA MELVYN DIDN'T WANT TO HAVE MAGIC LESSONS THE NEXT DAY OR the day after that. She said her head hurt, and she even sat in the recliner with a cloth over her eyes, but I think she was just upset that I wanted Cat to be in the act. I don't know why that bothered her, since she hadn't even met Cat. I decided to fix that and brought Cat home with me after school. Grandma Melvyn was watching *Wheel of Fortune* when we came into the family room. She looked at Cat's outfit: a T-shirt, a striped skirt, mismatched socks, and hiking boots.

"Hmmmph," Grandma Melvyn grunted.

Cat pulled a peanut butter and jelly taco out of her satchel and offered it to Grandma Melvyn.

"Want some?" she asked.

"You trying to poison me, Trixie?"

Cat laughed.

"Hmmmph," said Grandma Melvyn again and gave Cat the Wicked Wobble Eye.

Cat scrunched up her face and gave Grandma Melvyn her best impersonation of the Wicked Wobble Eye, though it was more of a Twinkly Blinky Eye. (Cat isn't good at wicked.)

"Hmmmph," Grandma Melvyn grunted again.

Cat laughed again. In case you hadn't noticed, she laughs a lot. That's one of the things I like about her. That and the way she doesn't let people bug her. And she doesn't judge people all the time. Cat figures that if someone is always cranky like Grandma Melvyn, it's just who they are. It doesn't mean they are a bad person.

Grandma Melvyn turned to the television and cranked up the volume. A skinny man with a bad haircut gave the giant wheel a spin and stared at the clue. It looked like this:

The man bit his lip nervously and shuffled his weight from one foot to the other like the future of the planet rested on it. He picked his letter.

"*L?*" he asked nervously.

"WHAT?" yelled Cat as she threw her taco at the television. "*Lizard* of Oz?!?!? Are you a moron?"

Grandma Melvyn looked at Cat with admiration. Yep, you heard me. Admiration.

"She'll do," Grandma Melvyn said.

And that was that. We resumed magic lessons the next day.

Grandma Melvyn taught me and Cat how to use the cabinet. I can't give away the illusion, but I can tell you that I was all wrong about how it worked. I can also tell you that the trick required two people and a hidden wooden lever. Remember that. It's important later.

I was wrong about something else, too. I thought Grandma Melvyn was a complainer, but she wasn't. Well, she *was*, but only about stupid things like the lawn, the house, food, television, fashion, vowels, and—well—the whole universe. Okay, Grandma Melvyn was a complainer, but she didn't complain about one thing: her knee.

Even though she didn't talk about her knee, I

could tell that something was wrong. She had stopped moving around like when she first got to our house. She was always waiting in the lawn chair when Cat and I got home, and she stayed there the whole afternoon. Sometimes, her knee hurt so much it gave her a headache and she sat in the recliner with a cloth over her eyes. Sometimes she drifted off to sleep mid-sentence. I think that was her body's way of dealing with the pain. It's not a big deal for most people to fall asleep in a chair, but it *is* a big deal when the person is Grandma Melvyn and *Wheel of Fortune* is on television.

CHAPTER 31

AFTER THE TACO-TOSSING INCIDENT, GRANDMA MELVYN WAS NICE TO CAT— by Grandma Melvyn standards. At least she didn't call her Trixie. She didn't call her Cat either. She just didn't call her anything. Coming from Grandma Melvyn, that was probably a compliment.

When we finished practice each day, Cat hung out with Grandma Melvyn and yelled at the Trixies on *Wheel of Fortune*. Grandma Melvyn didn't say much, but once, I caught her smiling while Cat laughed. It's easy to smile around Cat. Her laugh fills the whole room and makes you laugh from the inside all the way to the outside, even when you don't feel like it.

I think the woman in the black-and-white photographs at Grandma Melvyn's house was like that.

Her smile had power. I bet those Mount Rushmore presidents had a hard time keeping a straight face when she was around. And they were made of rock! The handsome man in the pictures didn't stand a chance.

I looked at Grandma Melvyn as she smiled at Cat, and I saw a peek of that woman. Grandma Melvyn kept her locked away, deep inside, but she was in there. Why did Grandma Melvyn keep her a prisoner in a cage of frowns and insults?

Was that the price of magic?

I KNOW THAT I'VE TOLD YOU THAT BEING PREPARED IS THE MOST IMPORTANT part of magic. And that expecting the unexpected is the most important part of magic. And that—well, you get the idea.

You know what else is the most important part of magic? Timing. As a magician, if your timing stinks, so do you. After Cat and I worked out the steps of the act, we had to practice, practice, practice to perfect the timing.

I think I need to tell you a little more about the act. Here's the summary:

I introduce Cat. She climbs into the cabinet. I close the panel, twirl the box three times, say some very magical words, perform some sleight of hand with my wand, and then presto chango . . . I open the panel and Cat is gone! I close the panel again, twirl the cabinet three times. Tap the mahogany with my wand and—*alakazam!* I open the panel again and Cat steps out. We grab hands, raise them high, and take an enormous bow to thunderous applause. *Ta-daaaa!*

That's how it's supposed to go. And you'll be thrilled to know that is exactly how it went in practice. You'll also be impressed to know that I stood up after my bow without knocking anything over or catching anything on fire. The act was scream free. Faint free. And fire department free. Perfect.

I was thrilled. Grandma Melvyn was not.

"Anybody can do that," she said. "You need pizzazz."

She pointed to a large, flat box tied with a deep red ribbon. I started to open it.

"Not for you!" Grandma Melvyn snapped. "For her!"

Cat untied the ribbon and retied it around her wrist like a bracelet.

"It's beautiful!" she said.

"You're as hopeless as he is," said Grandma Melvyn.

Cat opened the box and pulled out a red sequined hat with a tuft of red feathers.

"Now you're ready," said Grandma Melvyn.

Remember how I behaved when Grandma Melvyn agreed to let me use the cabinet? I just smiled like an idiot and said, "Thank you." Not Cat. She skipped right over to Grandma Melvyn and gave her a hug. Grandma Melvyn squirmed and tried to poke Cat with her cane, but she missed. And you know what? I think she missed on purpose.

Grandma Melvyn always has perfect aim.

CHAPTER 33

WE PRACTICED EVERY SPARE MINUTE WE HAD. THE CLOSER THE SHOW GOT, THE more excited I got. And I wasn't the only one. Cat and Grandma Melvyn were as excited as I was. There were a couple of times when I had to stay late at school for tutoring, but when I got home, Cat was already there with Grandma Melvyn.

Practice always makes magic acts better. But you can't practice forever. Eventually you run out of time. And that's what happened to us. Here was the timeline for the talent show:

1. Wednesday morning—bring all props to school for inspection. Principal Adolphus was very nervous about that. Surprise.

2. Friday after school: Talent Show Practice. Everyone

must attend. No exceptions. Period. This year, Principal Adolphus was playing it safe. He ordered the talent show run-through when he heard from every student in school—and half the city—that I had a new magic act. He said he needed to check out all the acts for safety and discipline purposes. I have a feeling that meant to check out *my* act for flying salamander purposes. That salamander had left a mark on Principal Adolphus. And not just the one on his forehead.

3. Saturday at five o'clock: All acts report to the auditorium.

4. Saturday at seven o'clock: Lights! Camera! Magic!

On Wednesday morning, Cat came by my house before school. We stashed my cape and wand and the red sequined hat inside the magician's cabinet, then covered the whole thing with a giant flowered sheet and rolled it to school. About two hundred kids ran by and half the buses drove past as we rolled the cabinet down the sidewalk, trying to dodge the deep cracks in the concrete. I can tell you one thing. You never notice how deep sidewalk cracks are until you try to roll an enormous sheet-covered magic cabinet over them. Everyone who passed by stared at us, and I could tell they were dying to know what was beneath that flowered sheet. Nate Watkins rode by on his bike, twisting his neck around like a turtle just to stare as he passed.

"Hey, Dorko," he yelled. "What's in the coffin? Your brains?"

Okay. That didn't even make sense, but I didn't care. I just ignored him. There was no way Nate "the Loser" Watkins was going to ruin my day. And besides, Nate got what was coming to him. He twisted around so much that he rode his bike right off the sidewalk and almost fell over. And you know what? I didn't even laugh. Much.

At school, Mr. Pierce, the janitor, opened the backstage door, and we hid the cabinet in the wings of the stage where no kids would bother it.

After we stashed the cabinet backstage, we went to class. Everybody was talking about us when we came in. The classroom sounded like a beehive again. *Buzzy. Buzz. Buzz. Buzz.* Cat grinned at me, but I kept a straight face. I tried to look cool, even though on the inside I was turning cartwheels. You can't buy press like that.

School was even more booooooorrrrrriiiiinnnngggg than usual. It took about twelve weeks for the day to end. Just before the final bell, Mrs. M passed out the tickets we had ordered for the talent show. I had requested seats near the front so Mom and Grandma Melvyn could have the best seats in the house. Dad was going to be in Shanghai, so he would miss it, but Mom would tape it so he could see it later. Mom cleared her calendar and everything. It was going to be awesome. In my mind, I added *The Great Hobson Talent Show* to our list of movies to watch on our next Movie Night. And we already have the candy!

I don't think Mrs. M was as excited about the talent show as I was. She handed me the ticket envelope with her patented I-don't-even-want-to-know-what-frightening-magical-extravaganza-you-have-dreamed-up-now look. (Mrs. M has very talented facial muscles.)

I opened the envelope. Front-row seats. This day could not get any better. I stuffed the tickets into my pocket, went straight home, and knocked on Grandma Melvyn's bedroom door.

You probably noticed that I didn't say "my bedroom" in that last sentence. The truth is that during the last couple of weeks, I had gotten used to Grandma Melvyn being around. And not just because of the magic lessons. But don't get me wrong. I still wanted my room back.

I guess that maybe I liked Grandma Melvyn. Just

a little. She wore her goofy jogging shoes with flashing lights in the heels and her sparkly sweatshirts from places like Niagara Falls and Atlantic City and Las Vegas. She stuck out, but she didn't apologize for it. In a way, Grandma Melvyn was like a dandelion in our perfect yard of zoysia grass.

There was one more thing about Grandma Melvyn. She had secrets. Things she wouldn't tell. When I asked her how she knew so much about magic, she asked me how I knew so much about minding my own business. The subject was off-limits, so I didn't push it. I figured she'd tell me when or if she was ready. Until then, I had tickets to share and a show to perform.

I opened the door to Grandma Melvyn's room.

And that's when everything went wrong.

CHAPTER 34

I PEEKED INSIDE.

"Grandma Melvyn?"

The room was empty. I was about to leave when I saw a black-and-white photo in a curlicue frame on the dresser. It was the missing photo from Grandma Melvyn's house. In the photo, two elegant wooden boxes stood in front of a black velvet curtain on a brightly lit stage. The face of a blond woman with dark lipstick and a toothy grin stuck out the end of one box, while her high-heeled shoes stuck out the end of the other box two yards away. She was sawed in half!

The handsome man and the round-freckled woman stood between the boxes holding hands. With her other hand, the woman held up a small saw. They were dressed up like movie stars and staring at each other like they were about to kiss or something. Blech.

I couldn't believe my eyes. I was looking at a picture of Grandma Melvyn and a real-life magician onstage! I was about to put it back on the dresser when a yellowed newspaper clipping fluttered to the floor. I picked it up as Grandma Melvyn stepped into the doorway behind me.

"What are you doing?"

I panicked and crammed the paper into my pocket with one hand and tried to put the picture back on the dresser with the other. It flew out of my hand and smashed against the corner of the dresser, then dropped to the floor in a shower of tiny glass triangles.

Grandma Melvyn and I both grabbed the broken frame, but as we stood up, the curlicue frame broke apart and the photograph ripped with a sickening sound. I let go and Grandma Melvyn looked at the destroyed picture in her hands.

"Get out," she said quietly.

"I . . ."

"Go away," she said in a whisper so soft I could barely hear it.

"I . . ."

"Go away . . . Trixie."

CHAPTER 35

HER WHISPER RANG IN MY EARS AS I RAN TO APE BOY'S ROOM AND TOOK Houdi from his cage. I climbed into the Hideout and sat there scratching Houdi behind the ears. My heart banged so loud I thought it would bust, but it wasn't loud enough to drown out that one whispered word . . .

Trixie.

Grandma Melvyn was right. I was a Trixie. I had destroyed the only photo she had cared enough about to bring from her house. The only photo with Grandma Melvyn and the handsome man. Together.

I pulled the newspaper clipping from my pocket and uncrumpled the fragile yellowed paper. The clipping was worn out from a thousand readings.

Surviving Magician Cancels Tour

The upcoming tour of internationally renowned magicians Martin and Melvyn was officially canceled today. The announcement was made one week after Giovanni Martin died in a one-car accident near Pecatonica, New York. The accident also claimed the life of his new bride, Trixie Monaghan. The couple had eloped on New Year's Eve and were married only three hours before the accident.

Strong winds and dangerous currents have hampered recovery efforts in the icy waters of Pecatonica Bay. The couple's bodies remain in their car, which skidded from the Bay Bridge early New Year's morning.

Trixie Monaghan of Port Washington had recently joined the long-running Martin and Melvyn magic act as an assistant and was set to tour with them this spring.

Angelica Melvyn was unavailable for comment.

I couldn't believe it. Grandma Melvyn was a magician, too. How could the handsome man run off and marry Trixie when he looked at Grandma Melvyn like he did in that picture? I didn't get it. Who would want to marry a Trixie instead of a real magician?

I bet Grandma Melvyn wondered that, too. How

many times had she read that article trying to figure it out? Trying to find a clue that she could never find because it was lost in the icy water of Pecatonica Bay.

Maybe that was the price of magic.

CHAPTER 36

SOMETIMES WHEN YOU HURT SOMEONE, YOU HAVE TO LEAVE THEM ALONE until they're ready to hear that you're sorry. Sometimes that's exactly the wrong thing to do, and you have to tell them right away, and if you don't, you just make it worse. And sometimes no matter what you do, the person *never ever, ever* wants to hear from you again, and nothing you try will help. Those are the times when you should just give up and join the French Foreign Legion. That's what they used to do in the old movies. If you've ever seen one, you'll know what I mean. Those movies always end with the guy crawling across the Sahara until he collapses and dies one sand dune from the fort. If you've seen those movies, you might have noticed that those French Foreign Legion guys always have canteens with them. They don't die of thirst. It's the guilt that kills them.

This was a French Foreign Legion situation, but I still had to try to tell Grandma Melvyn that I was sorry. And I really was sorry. I sat in the Hideout for three hours thinking of how to tell her, but my words were pathetic. And I know what you're thinking. Those were the easiest words in the world. Just say them already.

I. Am. Sorry.

How hard could that be? Impossible. That's how hard.

Those should be the easiest words in the English language, but I couldn't shake the image of Martin and Melvyn holding hands onstage, looking at each other like no one else in the whole world existed. I thought about the icy bridge and the skidding car. The screech of metal and terrified screams as the car plunged into freezing water with a horrible splash. Then silence.

Where was Grandma Melvyn when the call came that shattered her world? The call that left the beautiful

woman with the perfectly round freckle waiting . . .
waiting . . . waiting? Was she still waiting?

I am sorry should be the easiest thing in the world
to say, but sometimes *I am sorry* just doesn't cut it.

The problem is that sometimes it's all you've got.

CHAPTER 37

I WENT DOWN TO DINNER WITH A KNOT IN MY STOMACH, BUT GRANDMA Melvyn wasn't there. She had told Mom that her Trixiphobia was flaring up and stayed in her room the rest of the night. I wrote a pathetic note telling her how sorry I was. I put it into an envelope with her ticket for the magic show and slid it under her door. Half a second later, the unopened envelope slid back into the hall. Grandma Melvyn wasn't ready to hear from me. Time to get a canteen.

The next morning, I went to the kitchen hoping that Grandma Melvyn would be there with her cane so she could trip me with it. She wasn't. Mom was there, stuffing peanut butter sandwiches into lunch boxes for me and Ape Boy. She was in a major rush.

"Is Grandma Melvyn okay?" I asked.

"Why wouldn't she be?" Mom asked, but she didn't wait for an answer. "While I think of it, I need you to make sure Grandma Melvyn takes her meds after school. I've got a meeting, so I won't be home. Can you do that?"

Before I could inform Mom that Grandma Melvyn wouldn't be taking meds or anything from me for the next two hundred years, Mom hugged me and ran out the door.

I grabbed my lunch box and backpack and left Grandma Melvyn's envelope on the kitchen table with three peanut butter cups (Grandma Melvyn's favorite) and went to school.

Nothing interesting happened at school all day. And even if it did, I wouldn't have noticed. I was too busy thinking about Grandma Melvyn's photograph and trying to figure out how I could make it up to her even though I knew there was no way I could. The longer I thought about it, the worse I felt.

What do you call a whole bunch of knots tangled together? A noodle of knots? A caboodle? Knot-a-lot? I don't know, but by the time I got home at around four o'clock, I had one in my stomach. It felt like a whole family of boa constrictors twisting around, trying to squeeze one another to death.

The envelope and peanut butter cups were still on the table when I got home and Grandma Melvyn's door was wide open, but she was not inside. Grandma Melvyn was gone. Her suitcase was gone. Her pillow was gone. Everything Grandma Melvyn had brought to our house was gone.

Except for a tiny triangle of glass at the foot of the dresser, there was no sign that she had been there at all.

It was first-grade math to figure out where she had gone. I grabbed the key from the cupboard, got out my bike, and started toward Grandma Melvyn's house.

It was hot outside—more like June than March. After two blocks, I was sweating like a dog, and not one of those little bald Chihuahuas, either. I was sweating like a big, hairy Saint Bernard in a sauna. At the equator. During the summer. And, yeah, I know it's always summer at the equator. I'm just trying to draw you a picture. Not a pretty one, is it?

After three blocks, I found Grandma Melvyn's pillow lying beside the sidewalk. I picked it up, balanced it on my handlebars and kept going. In the next block,

I found her knit hat on a lilac bush and stuffed it into the pillowcase. A block later, I found her Windbreaker. Then a sock . . . then her other sock . . . her VIVA LAS VEGAS sweatshirt . . . her sweatpants. Block after block, I scooped up the clothes, stuffed them into the pillowcase, and kept biking toward her house. I only hoped I wouldn't find Grandma Melvyn walking along in nothing but her birthday suit. (And I don't mean the purple one she bought in Atlantic City last year.)

At last, I saw Grandma Melvyn sitting on the bottom porch step of her house in an ELVIS LIVES! T-shirt, jogging shorts, and her flashing jogging shoes. Grandma Melvyn wearing clothes was good. Grandma Melvyn's knee was horrible. Her knee looked like a bright pink cantaloupe. She sat with her leg propped up on her huge roly-poly suitcase.

I dropped my bike on the grass and ran over to her. Grandma Melvyn awkwardly covered her knee with her hand and gave me a Wicked Wobble Eye that could melt iron.

"Are you okay?" I asked.

"Get lost," she said.

"I'm going to call Mom," I said. "Let me help you inside."

"I like it fine right here," she said.

"Please, let me get you some ice," I said.

"I don't need Trixie. I don't need ice. And I don't need you," she said.

"I'm calling Mom," I said.

I set the pillowcase on the step and went to the door, but it was locked. Grandma Melvyn hadn't even been inside. She had rolled her fat red suitcase ten blocks in the hot sun with a bad knee and couldn't even climb the stairs to get inside her own house when she got there.

I pulled the spare key from my pocket and unlocked the door. Then I called Mom from the old-fashioned black telephone on the narrow table in the hall. It took forever for the rotary dial to slowly click out the numbers. I wound the thick phone cord around my index finger over and over while I stared at my feet to avoid looking at the curlicue-shaped patch of sad blue paint on the wall. Mom was in a meeting, and I had to get her out of it to tell her about Grandma Melvyn. I thought she'd be really mad, but she said she'd come right away.

I got a glass of water and a bag of frozen peas from the freezer, then I went outside and gently set the bag of peas onto Grandma Melvyn's knee. She gasped and jerked back in pain.

"I'm sorry," I said.

She didn't say anything. She repositioned the peas and closed her eyes.

"I'm sorry for everything," I said, sitting on the step beside her.

Grandma Melvyn roughly grabbed the glass from my hand, splashing my arm with cold water. I wiped off my arm as Grandma Melvyn pulled off her glasses. I looked away as she dried the drops of water that had somehow splashed behind her glasses into her eyes.

We sat silently on the step until Mom drove up and backed the car into the driveway. She helped Grandma Melvyn into the front seat while I locked the house and loaded Grandma Melvyn's things into the trunk. Grandma Melvyn sat stiffly in the passenger seat as Mom stretched the belt over her body and clicked the buckle. Mom closed the door and got into the driver's seat and started the car.

As they drove down the street, Grandma Melvyn stared in the car mirror at the dork with his bike standing in a patch of dandelions. At last, the car turned the corner and was gone.

CHAPTER 38

THAT NIGHT, I DREAMED THAT I HIT GRANDMA MELVYN WITH MY BICYCLE. SHE was standing on the sidewalk in front of her house and I tried to stop, but I couldn't. I plowed right into her knee, and it swelled up like a balloon about to pop. The worst part was that she didn't yell or scream or anything. She just looked at me and whispered, ". . . Trixie."

I woke up and tried to think of something else, but I couldn't. After a while, I fell asleep again, but it took a long time, and when I had to get up for school, I was so tired and slow that Mom had to drive me so I wouldn't be late. School dragged all day, but at least it was Friday and there was an assembly in the gym for the last two periods. The whole school heard a lecture and watched a movie about dental hygiene. To answer your questions: 1. Yes, it involved actors dressed like toothbrushes. 2. Yes, it was as boring as it sounds.

I should have hated it, but I didn't mind at all because it gave me a chance to sleep. Besides, Cat was gone, so I didn't have anybody to laugh at the movie with. I wondered where she was. She had been in line behind me when we left the classroom, but she never made it to the gym. Everyone went back to class for ten minutes before the final bell, but Cat wasn't there, either. I know that Cat can flake out, but this was a bad time to do it.

When the bell rang, all the kids in the talent show went to the auditorium for mandatory practice. I wasn't in the mood for it. I wasn't even sure Grandma Melvyn would still let me use the cabinet in the talent show, and I wouldn't blame her if she didn't—though I still hoped she would.

I still wanted to show the world what I could do, but that didn't seem so important anymore. Now I had another reason to perform my act. I wanted to show Grandma Melvyn what I had learned from her and to thank her. Maybe that would help her feel better. Just a little. Maybe it would show that she was important to someone. To me.

I went to the auditorium to get ready for rehearsal. Cat wasn't there, either. Remember when I said that the practice was required for everyone, no exceptions? If she didn't show up before our turn, we would be out of the show. I sat in the auditorium seats waiting with the other performers until our turn.

Talent show practice wasn't much of a practice, because none of the dancers danced and none of the singers sang. (Which, come to think about it, is a lot like the actual show.)

Practice was teaching everyone how to line up. If you think it's easy to line up kids, you've never been in a school. It took half an hour just to line up the kindergartners. It was like herding a bunch of baby goats. I guess that was appropriate, since they both smell funky and try to eat everything they see.

Cat and I were the final act in the lineup. You're probably thinking that's because they wanted to save the best for last. It's not. They were trying to keep parents happy. Last year, my act was in the middle of the show. When the fire marshal closed down the show after me, a whole bunch of second-grade dancers had nowhere to show off their moves. (Note to last year's audience: You're welcome.)

I was starting to worry that Cat wasn't going to make it and we'd be kicked out of the show. Finally, she came running through the auditorium door, plopped into the seat beside me, and smiled. She didn't even say sorry or anything. I should have been mad, but I was just glad to see her.

Principal Adolphus looked at me.

"I'd like you to run through your whole act," he said. "You know, just to see how it goes."

You might think it was unfair for me and Cat to run through our whole act when nobody else had to, but it was okay. I didn't mind the practice.

Everyone paid extra close attention when we took the stage. Before we started, Principal Adolphus checked out the cabinet—just in case. And he checked it out after—just in case. And can I tell you? All the other kids clapped! Our trick worked perfectly. No flying amphibians. No high-pitched screams from Mr. Adolphus. No firefighters. No problem.

We were in the show.

CHAPTER 39

GRANDMA MELVYN'S KNEE LOOKED A LITTLE BETTER ON SATURDAY MORNING, but Mom took her to the doctor just to make sure that she hadn't done any damage to it. He said she hadn't, and he had some other good news, too. The insurance company was going to pay for her knee replacement surgery. He scheduled her for the operation in ten days.

While Mom and Grandma Melvyn were at the doctor's, I grabbed the twenty-six dollars I'd saved for a top hat and biked downtown to find something for Grandma Melvyn. I couldn't un-tear the photo or fix the frame. I couldn't fix her leg. I couldn't fix anything, really, but maybe I could cheer Grandma Melvyn up a little. Maybe I could do something to show her I was sorry.

I knew it was going to be tough, but finding something for Grandma Melvyn turned out to be impossible. I went into both department stores downtown and the three antique shops, but I couldn't find anything that inspired me. On my way home, I stopped at the big drugstore on Cherokee Street. It had everything. And I mean *everything*, including an aisle just for weird products from TV, like the Weed-Whack-i-nator and Monkey Snuggies. You know the stuff. I looked at all of it, but nothing said "Grandma Melvyn" to me. It did say, "People have too much money and free time and probably should turn off the TV and read a book once in a while."

I walked up and down the aisles and found everything from pudding to Pampers. Glue to glitter. Candy to canes. I bought three of those items and biked home. Hint: I did *not* buy candy, pudding, or Pampers. Secret confession: I *did* buy candy, but I ate it on the way home, so I'm not including it in the list.

You probably think you know what happened next. You probably think I went to the kitchen, spread some newspapers on the table, used the glue to draw a beautiful geometric design on the cane, and sprinkled it with glitter, creating a unique and magnificent work of art perfect for any aging ex-magician who loves pizzazz.

Shows what you know.

I went to the kitchen, spread newspapers on the table, and used the glue to draw a line, which made it look like a Labrador retriever with a gluey tongue had licked the cane. I scraped away as much of the extra glue as I could and changed my design.

Remember what I said about always having a plan B in magic? It's a good idea for art, too. Since my beautiful geometric design wasn't going to work, I changed it to a beautiful bouquet of flowers with a green stem.

I sprinkled green glitter over the cane. The glitter stuck. It stuck to the line, which was nice. It stuck to my gluey thumbprints, which was not. It stuck to every drip and dribble. It stuck to everything. I tried to brush away the extra glitter, and it stuck to my hands. To my arms. To my face, my shoes, my teeth, my . . . You get the picture.

That's when I learned one of the most ancient laws of the universe: Glitter is evil.

The cane was a disaster. The kitchen was a disaster. My face was a disaster. Before I could figure out what to do next, Mom and Grandma Melvyn opened the front door. I scooped up the newspaper and cane, opened the door to the garage, and tossed everything inside. Glitter snowed down inside the garage like it was Christmas on Mars.

I slammed the door shut as Mom and Grandma stepped into the kitchen. Grandma Melvyn leaned on her cane with one hand and Mom's arm with the other. She swayed back and forth and hummed to herself.

"Just a few more steps," said Mom. "Then you can nap a bit."

"What's wrong with Grandma Melvyn?" I asked.

"She got a shot at the doctor's office," Mom said, "and it's making her drowsy."

"Can I help?" I asked.

Mom looked at the glitter-bombed kitchen and my glittery smile and sighed.

"Yeah," she said. "You can clean up your mess."

I followed them to the family room and helped Grandma Melvyn settle into the recliner. I covered her with a small blanket (and a significant amount of glitter). Grandma Melvyn looked at me like I was out of focus.

"A leprechaun," she said. "That's nice. Trixie didn't tell me we had leprechauns."

Grandma Melvyn patted my sparkly green hand, closed her eyes, and drifted to sleep. Maybe I helped Grandma Melvyn feel better after all.

CHAPTER 40

GRANDMA MELVYN SLEPT IN THE RECLINER ALL AFTERNOON WHILE I unsuccessfully attacked the glitter in the kitchen and then got ready for the talent show. I found sparkles in places that should never sparkle, and I don't mean the kitchen.

By the time I got cleaned up, it was already six o'clock. I was supposed to be at school an hour ago, and I still hadn't eaten anything. In fact, I realized I hadn't eaten anything since breakfast. I was suddenly starving. I went to the kitchen and snarfed down a bowl of Lucky Charms cereal. Magically delicious.

Time was ticking, but I had one more thing to do before I got out of the house. I still had not done anything to tell Grandma Melvyn that I was sorry. I knew that sooner or later she would wake up from her nap, and I wanted her to know that at least I had tried. I wrote on the back of Grandma Melvyn's ticket: "Dedicated to the Amazing Melvyn. I am sorry. —Robbie."

I checked on Grandma Melvyn. Part of me hoped that she would be awake and would want to come to the show. The rest of me was afraid that she would be awake and not want to come to the show.

It didn't matter. Grandma Melvyn was still asleep, with her glasses on the table next to the chair. I had never seen her without her glasses, and for the first time, I looked closely at her creased face. Instead of the lion tamer or a world-famous magician, Grandma Melvyn was just a tiny old woman snuggled beneath a glittery blanket, her thin cheeks puffing in and out as she snored softly. I quietly put the ticket and a peanut butter cup on Grandma Melvyn's blanket.

Grandma Melvyn wasn't going to make it to the show, but at least Mom and Ape Boy would be there to tape it. I could show it to Grandma Melvyn, and maybe Cat could come over to watch, too.

It wasn't perfect, but it would have to do.

CHAPTER 41

MOM WAS STANDING BY THE KITCHEN SINK, TALKING ON HER CELL PHONE.

"Can you drive me to school?" I asked.

She waved her hand at me.

"Look . . . No. That won't work!" she snapped at the person on the other end of the call. "No! I'm telling you the rate is wrong."

Mom was annoyed. She paced back and forth. I tapped her arm to get her attention. I was already late and had to get to the school before the show began. Mom raised her finger to tell me to wait.

"I said I'd get it done," she said. "E-mail the numbers now."

I tapped her arm again.

"I have to go NOW!" I said.

Mom put her hand over the phone.

"Just hold on," she said, and then put the phone up to her ear again.

I didn't have time to hold on. I was late and Mom didn't even care.

That's when Ape Boy came into the room and climbed onto a chair. His hand was stuck inside a giant orange bag of candy. Reese's Pieces.

"Hey!" I yelled. "Those are for me and Mom!"

"Shhhh," Mom said. "Not you . . . I'm talking to my kids."

Mom snapped her fingers at us and signaled for us to be quiet.

I grabbed the bag from Ape Boy, but he grabbed it back and the plastic bag ripped apart. Reese's Pieces flew through the air like tiny orange, yellow, and brown hailstones.

"Mom!" Ape Boy screamed.

"Where'd you find that bag?"

"Mom gave it to me!" yelled Ape Boy.

"You liar," I said. "She wouldn't do that. It's for Movie Night."

Mom put her hand up to silence me. She tapped her watch face with her finger and pointed angrily at the door.

"Seven percent is the wrong rate . . . ," she said, and walked out of the room.

My face burned with anger, and I ran out the door and slammed it behind me. I ran down the street and cut through the field toward the school, kicking clumps of grass as I ran.

When I got to school, I was really late, but Cat was waiting for me by the flagpole. I kicked the flagpole and it made a loud echoey clanging noise.

"Hey there," she said.

I didn't say anything.

"It looks like a good crowd," she said.

Silence.

We should already have gotten our stuff from the cabinet and headed to the library to wait for our turn to go onstage. Cat knew that, and she could have gone to the library without me, but she didn't.

Instead, she kicked the flagpole.

Clang!

"That's awesome," she said, and kicked it again and laughed. "Watch this."

She pulled her fist way back like a Rock 'Em Sock 'Em Robot punching a wall or something. Then she fake-punched my arm and kicked the flagpole at the same time.

Clang!

Cat burst out laughing and did it again.

Clang! Clang!

"Hey!" I said.

I was mad and I wanted to stay mad.

Clang! Clang!

A tiny laugh bubbled up inside me.

Clang! Clang!

The laugh fought its way up through my gut and popped out my mouth. Cat smiled. I kicked the pole and "punched" her back.

Clang! Clang!

Cat grinned.

"Let's go put on a magic show," she said.

I gave the pole one last kick and followed her into the school.

Principal Adolphus was onstage welcoming people to the show when Cat and I sneaked backstage and got our gear out of the cabinet. It was off to the side of the stage, so nobody could see us, but we could peek out at the audience. It was hard to see beyond the first ten rows, but the auditorium seemed full. Except for three empty seats in the front. My face got hot. Mom hadn't even tried to get there.

Just then the audience clapped as two first-grade girls with ponytails stepped onto the stage and walked up to the microphone, which was nine inches above their heads. Mrs. Thompson, the music teacher, rushed onstage and lowered the microphone, then walked to the piano. She gave them a big nod and began to play.

The girls stood like statues staring at the crowd, but when Mrs. Thompson played the piano introduction for the third time, they started to sing. They squeezed each other's hands like they might drown if they let go. The girls sang so quietly, I could barely hear them—even with microphones—but it didn't matter. When they finished, they hugged each other and jumped up and down and squealed while the crowd clapped and cheered. Finally, Mrs. Thompson shuffled them offstage. Cat smiled and clapped for them.

Seeing her enthusiasm reminded me that this show was important to her, too. Even if I had ruined things with Grandma Melvyn and even if Mom didn't come, I owed it to Cat to do my best. It was time to put on a show and to give it my all, because there really wasn't another option. I think we settled that way back in Chapter 1. Cat grabbed Grandma Melvyn's red sequined hat, and I took my cape and wand, and we walked to the library.

The library was packed with dancers, singers, gymnasts, violinists, laundry ninjas, and Dancing Chicken Butts. Don't ask. One by one, the acts were called backstage, where they waited for their turn to perform. We watched the show on a monitor in the library. Some of the acts were amazing, like the kid with the Chinese yo-yo. And the girl who solved a Rubik's Cube blindfolded. After a while I quit watching and ran through our act in my mind. I had to concentrate very hard to block out the feelings that kept creeping back up inside me. I tried visualizing my act in my mind. That's a very important technique in magic. At least for me. Cat didn't bother visualizing; she sat in the corner and read a book.

Finally, the library was empty except for us and the Dancing Chicken Butts. It was our turn to line up. Cat and I walked (and the Chicken Butts waddled) to the backstage door and lined up in the wings. As the Chicken Butts took the stage, I peeked at the audience from behind the black velvet drapes.

Two second-grade boys sat in the front row seats reserved for someone else. Someone who was supposed to be there taping the show. Someone who was not.

At last, the Dancing Chicken Butts took a bow and waddled offstage. One of the PTA volunteers rolled Grandma Melvyn's cabinet center stage as whispers rose from the audience. Even after three hours of bad dancing, awful singing, laundry ninjas, and Dancing Chicken Butts, the auditorium was packed. Everyone had stayed to the bitter end waiting for our act. They were hoping either to see the greatest magic act ever or to tape the winning entry for *America's Stupidest Videos*. One way or the other, they would get what they came for. I took a deep breath as Principal Adolphus stepped to the microphone.

"And finally," he said, "it's Robert Darko and Cat Mulligan!"

Whispers swelled in the auditorium as the crowd fidgeted and squirmed in their seats to get a better view of the stage. There was no polite applause like when the other acts came onstage. Just the familiar buzzing of bees. I was glad that Houdi wasn't there. My mouth felt like it was stuffed with cotton, and my heart pounded. I looked at Cat, who blew a feather out of her face and gave me a wimpy smile. I wanted to step onstage, but my feet would not move.

Principal Adolphus waved us onto the stage, shuffling nervously. His face turned red, and the vein in his neck bulged out even more than it had that day in his office.

"Robert Darko and Cat Mulligan!" he said even louder.

Instantly, the whispers stopped. Complete silence filled the auditorium. I swallowed hard. This was it. The chance I had waited for to show Hobson Elementary School and the world what I could do. I took another deep breath and grabbed Cat's hand, and we stepped into the bright lights of the Hobson Elementary School auditorium.

Showtime!

CHAPTER 42

"LADIES AND GENTLEMEN," I SAID, "WE ARE STANDING BESIDE THE LEGENDARY Chamber of Dimensions, made famous by the renowned magicians Martin and Melvyn. It is not only beautiful, but it is also full of—"

"Salamanders?" yelled a voice suspiciously like that of Nate Watkins, fifth-grade loser.

"MAGIC!" I yelled back. "It's full of magic! The Chamber of Dimensions has the power to magically transport a person into another dimension! The *next* dimension!" I paused for effect, then I twirled the cabinet three times and said the magic word.

"Open, salamand—sesame! Open, sesame!"

I flourished my cape to distract the audience while Cat flipped the hidden wooden lever on the side of the cabinet. The panel popped open. The audience clapped politely.

Cat took my hand, and I spun her around while she smiled and waved. It was a pretty good dance move. She stepped into the box and waved again.

"Into the *next* dimension!" I said, and closed the panel.

I spun the cabinet around three times, waved my wand dramatically, and tossed a fistful of green glitter into the air, distracting the audience while I flipped the lever again.

Presto! The cabinet opened, and it was empty! The audience clapped more enthusiastically.

"Return to our dimension!"

I closed the door, spun the cabinet, and waved my wand again. I looked at the audience. Cat smiled at me from the front row.

I twirled the cabinet around one more time.

Wait . . . What?

Cat waved from a seat that had been empty a minute before. A seat that should not in any possible scenario contain the person who was supposed to be waiting for me to say some magic words and bring her back from the next dimension, which—for the record—

is *not* the first row of the Hobson Elementary School auditorium.

"Uh . . . ," I said. "I . . ."

Cat pointed at the cabinet and mouthed the words *open it.*

"Uh . . . ," I said.

Cat pointed at the box again. I waved my right hand dramatically and secretly flipped the lever with my left hand.

The panel swung open, and out stepped Grandma Melvyn in the red feathered hat and a glittery sequined gown hanging loosely over her Niagara Falls sweatshirt. The long, sparkling gown flowed over her light-up jogging shoes into a glittery puddle of fabric. Grandma Melvyn took a gigantic bow, sparkling from her hat to her green glittery cane. The crowd cheered wildly.

When she stood up, Grandma Melvyn stood ten feet taller than I had ever seen her before, and she was smiling. Her smile filled the whole auditorium. It filled the whole world.

I was stunned. I stood there with my mouth wide open, looking like the biggest dork in the universe, but nobody noticed. Every single eye in the auditorium was on Grandma Melvyn. She waved elegantly, then twirled around and took another bow.

She poked me with her glittery green cane and whispered, "Watch and learn, Robbie Darko. Watch and learn."

Grandma Melvyn pulled a bouquet of daisies from my pocket and tossed it to the audience. She twirled around and turned a handkerchief into a dove. She raised her hand and sent the dove soaring gracefully over the audience. The crowd went wild. Grandma Melvyn took off her sequined hat and tossed it into the air. It vanished in a flash of light and a puff of smoke.

Bravo!

I stood on the stage with my mouth still open, watching Grandma Melvyn do her stuff. That's when I learned what it meant to be a real magician. It had nothing to do with tricks or props. It had everything to do with love. Grandma Melvyn wasn't up there to prove anything to anyone. She was there because she loved magic, and even though Grandma Melvyn didn't like people very much, she loved the audience. And because of that, they loved her and believed everything she did. They were rooting for her. They wanted to believe. She made them feel that.

Grandma Melvyn twirled and swirled around the stage, gracefully performing trick after trick, pausing only long enough to strike a pose and acknowledge the audience's love. She owned the stage, and she was amazing.

She was Grandma Melvyn.

CHAPTER 43

AT LAST, GRANDMA MELVYN STEPPED TO THE MICROPHONE AND RAISED HER hand to hush the audience. Silence swept over the auditorium.

"And now, ladies and gentlemen," she said, "we will perform a trick so daring and dangerous no one has performed it in half a century! I know, because it was last performed by me!"

Cat stepped onstage carrying a long, narrow wooden box. Grandma Melvyn opened the box and pulled out two sword-length sewing needles threaded with long white satin ribbons. Cat closed the box and stepped back into the wings of the stage while Grandma Melvyn thrust the needles into the air like Joan of Arc on the battlefield. The piercing-sharp needles glinted in the stage lights, and the white coils of ribbon flashed through the air like striking snakes.

I heard a gasp from the audience.

"However, to perform this daring and dangerous act," Grandma Melvyn said, "I need a volunteer."

Grandma Melvyn pointed a needle at the audience and waved it back and forth as if the needle had the power to pick the perfect victim. It waved left, then right, then left again . . . slowly . . . slowly . . . then *zoom!* The needle swung around and pointed straight at Principal Adolphus.

That's when everything slipped into slow motion just like in the movies. A word screamed in my mind but could not find my mouth in time to be heard by anyone else.

Nooooooooo—

I could tell by the look of terror in his eyes that Principal Adolphus was moving in slow motion, too. His brain was reliving the terrors of Talent Shows Past. Yet he was powerless against Grandma Melvyn's tractor beam needle. It pulled him across the stage like a zombie. He stopped in front of the cabinet. Grandma Melvyn handed me the needles and swept the principal into the cabinet, slamming the panel shut behind him.

"Welcome to the big time," she whispered to me as Cat stepped out of the wings and struck a pose that directed the attention of everyone in the entire universe right at me.

Wait! What?

Grandma Melvyn smiled as I clutched the sewing needles and waited in the blinding glare of a million eyes without a single clue what to do next.

CHAPTER 44

REMEMBER WHEN I TOLD YOU GRANDMA MELVYN TAUGHT ME HOW TO USE THE cabinet and showed me things it could do that I hadn't figured out before? I remember that day, too. What I don't remember is two swordlike needles with yards and yards of white satin ribbon. I think I would have remembered that, don't you?

I stood there with a gigantic needle in each hand and the whole world watching while I tried to figure out what to do next. It might have been okay if time had remained in slow motion, but it didn't. Time picked up speed until it zoomed by in a blur. And not just for me. It must have done that for Principal Adolphus, too. From inside the box, Principal Adolphus yelled and knocked on the wood like an angry woodpecker.

"Mrmbmmmrmvkm fmfmmrmmsmlrm!"

You don't need to be fluent in Angry Principal to know what he was saying. Seconds ticked past as I stood there. My brain jumped from the needles to the box to the audience and back again. Then I looked at Grandma Melvyn. The look on her face said, "Be amazing." And so I was. Because sometimes you just have to be. What else are you going to do? Be a flop?

I lifted the needles high into the air and crossed them above my head and then swished them around like an ancient sword master. I really didn't know what to do with them, but I was going to fake it until I figured it out. The ribbons snapped through the air as I dramatically circled the box. I moved like I was casting a spell. Once around the box. Twice around the box. Three times around . . .

And then I knew what to do!

I pushed the needle into one of the oval holes at the side of the box. It slid into the box on one side, and the brilliant point jabbed out of a hole on the opposite side. In a heartbeat, Grandma Melvyn stepped around to the glinting point and gracefully pulled the needle from the box. The ribbon trailed behind it, transformed from brilliant white to blood red.

The audience cheered. Grandma Melvyn raised her needle and shot a glance at the second needle in my hand. I raised it high, and then, as if we had practiced a million times, we each jabbed our needles into the box and threaded the ribbons back and forth, back and forth through the holes, until the white tail ends of the ribbons dangled from my side of the box and the two silver needles dangled from twelve inches of red ribbon on her side. We only got tangled up two or three times, but not for long, so I don't think the audience ever noticed. We twirled the box around three times, and I knocked on the front of the cabinet while Grandma Melvyn prepared to flip the wooden lever. The panel opened, and there it was . . .

The moment with no name. When anything is possible and everyone holds their breath and waits to see what comes next.

The funny thing is, I didn't really know what was supposed to happen next. In a way, I was experiencing it with the audience. Only closer. We looked inside the box. It was filled with a web of blood-red ribbons. The principal was gone!

Grandma Melvyn grabbed my hand and raised it high into the air, and the crowd went wild. Then

Grandma Melvyn stepped back and directed the attention to me. I stood there with the clapping audience, flashing cameras, beaming stage lights, and a smiling Grandma Melvyn, and I took the biggest bow of my life.

"Ta-daaaa!"

You probably think everything went perfectly after that and people were thrilled and Principal Adolphus proclaimed Hobson Elementary School an International Magic Sanctuary or something cool like that. And you know what? If this was a movie, that's exactly what would have happened. The other thing that would have happened is that Grandma Melvyn's dove would have dive-bombed Nate Watkins or dropped a load on his head, if you know what I mean. Insert major sound effect here! However, this is not a movie—yet—so none of those things happened. Here's what did happen.

After I took the biggest bow of my life—and stood up again without catching anything on fire—I closed the panel, and Grandma Melvyn and I unlaced the box by threading the needles back through the holes. When the ribbons were loose, we twirled the box three times, knocked three times on the front—three is the magic number, in case you hadn't noticed—and then I flipped the wooden lever, which broke off in my hand.

Oops.

Of course, we did exactly what magicians are supposed to do in that situation. We smiled. The audience didn't know anything was wrong, and we weren't about to show it. Grandma Melvyn and I smiled, dramatically waved our hands, and twirled the box some more.

Eventually, people started to suspect that something was wrong. The high-pitched screams from inside the box were probably their first clue. When the janitor walked onstage with a crowbar and a hatchet, the act was over.

"Don't break the cabinet!" I yelled.

I felt a hand on my arm. It was Grandma Melvyn.

"Sometimes, Robbie," she said, "you've got to let things go."

Then she smiled and tucked her cool, wrinkled hand into the crook of my arm and led me from the stage of the Hobson Elementary Talent Show.

She never looked back.

CHAPTER 45

GRANDMA MELVYN AND I STEPPED INTO THE CROWDED HALLWAY WHERE parents were trying to find their kids and get home. The kids just wanted to run up and down the hallways screaming. It was chaos. One of the singing girls with ponytails asked Grandma Melvyn for her autograph. Grandma Melvyn beamed as she signed the girl's talent show program, then she pulled a coin out of the girl's ear. The girl clapped and reached for the quarter, but just like that, it vanished.

"Do I look like a bank?" Grandma Melvyn said. "Go mooch money off your parents."

The girl ran away.

Cat was waiting for us next to a talent show poster. She punched me in the arm, then gave Grandma

Melvyn the biggest hug I've ever seen, and you know what? Grandma Melvyn didn't even complain about it.

"We did it!" Cat yelled.

"Not bad," Grandma Melvyn said. "Not as good as Toronto in '67. I knocked 'em dead in '67."

"Were you surprised, Robbie?" asked Cat. "You didn't even know Grandma Melvyn and I were practicing when you weren't around, did you? That's where I was during the assembly yesterday!"

Mystery solved.

Grandma Melvyn looked down the hall as if she was trying to find someone.

"Where's Trixie?" she said. "She was supposed to be here when we came offstage."

"Which Trixie?" I asked.

"The one who spends all her time working so you can play magician," said Grandma Melvyn. "Who do you think?"

I didn't understand.

"Mom didn't come," I said.

"Shows what you know," said Grandma Melvyn. "Get your nose out of your top hat and pay more attention."

My cheeks burned, but Grandma Melvyn chuckled.

"Don't work yourself into a wedgie," she said. "You're still young."

Grandma Melvyn leaned on the green cane and started down the hallway. She stopped after a couple of steps and waved the cane at me. Flecks of glitter snowed onto the glossy white floor tiles.

"You'd better stick with magic," she said. "You'll never make it as a cane designer."

CHAPTER 46

I FOLLOWED GRANDMA MELVYN DOWN THE HALLWAY TO THE MAIN ENTRANCE
of the school. Mom was waiting by the office in a crowd of
noisy parents. A knot of snakes twisted in my stomach
when I saw her. It was first-grade math to figure out
why she wasn't in her seat at the show. She had been
too busy helping Ape Boy and Grandma Melvyn *and*
cleaning up candy messes to get there on time. Mom
looked tired.

"Mom," I said. "I . . ."

Mom didn't say anything. She wrapped her arms
around me and hugged me tight. Then she leaned back
and looked at me.

"You were magnificent, kiddo," she said, blinking
away tears. "Just magnificent."

She hugged me again until someone yelled something about a kid climbing a flagpole. Then Mom laughed and let go.

"C'mon," she said. "Let's get your brother down and grab a treat on the way home."

We bought a box of chocolate cupcakes with white squiggles and a gallon of chocolate milk and ate them at the kitchen table. Dad called from Shanghai to hear about the show, and I told him all about it. Except the part about the janitor and the hatchet. Hey, I didn't want to ruin all the surprises. I hate spoilers.

Eventually, Mom and Ape Boy went to bed, but Grandma Melvyn and I stayed in the kitchen. The day hadn't started out so well, but it ended up being the best day of my life, and I wanted it to last forever. Grandma Melvyn was too busy to go to bed. Her brain was on fire with ideas for her new act. A new act with her new assistant. Guess who!

Yep. It's me. But don't worry about Cat. Grandma Melvyn said there was plenty of assisting to go around and that Cat could help, too.

Grandma Melvyn worked like she was on a mission, making up for lost time. She sat at the table doodling in a battered spiral notebook. She sketched a cabinet with a big wheel on the door. Here was the idea: A member of the audience would spin the wheel and the assistant in the cabinet would turn into a bird or a cat or a beach ball or whatever else the wheel decided. Between you and me, I think she got that idea from *Wheel of Fortune*, but it didn't matter, because she crossed out the whole picture, flipped the page, and started over.

"Levitation!" she said. "That's the thing."

She sketched a new cabinet and covered it with tangled arrows showing where she and I would move and what we would do. After about thirty seconds, it looked like a bowl of spaghetti.

"No, no, no!" she snapped, crossing out the drawing.

"We need a hook," she said. "Grab those Trixies by the collars and don't let go!"

We sat together in the circle of light from the lamp above the kitchen table. The world beyond was dark and silent. I watched Grandma Melvyn doodle and think and talk to herself and doodle and think some more. Every couple of minutes, she tilted her notebook to show me her latest idea, and almost as fast she pulled it away, crossed it out, and started over.

Maybe it was the long, long day catching up with me, or maybe there was something calming about watching Grandma Melvyn work, but as I sat at the table and the shadows edged closer and closer, I relaxed and my body got heavier and heavier, and I rested my head on my arm, and it was so comfortable. I watched Grandma Melvyn draw and think and scribble ideas and flip pages and start over, her voice swirling through the air like a faraway song, faint and familiar and just out of reach. Once in a while, her words found me, then her voice faded again.

. . . stand right there . . . levitate . . .

I breathed deeply and slowly.

. . . maybe a lever . . . signal . . .

I blinked and blinked again, and I closed my eyes one last time—

. . . Thank you, Robbie . . .

—and I slept.

CHAPTER 47

I WASN'T KIDDING WHEN I SAID THAT GRANDMA MELVYN WAS LIKE A WOMAN on a mission, making up for lost time. By Sunday evening, she had filled her notebook with scratched-out doodles and started a new one. She was serious about putting together a new act, and on Monday, we started training. We practiced card tricks and close-up magic and talked about Grandma Melvyn's next big act. No matter how hard I worked, she worked twice as hard. Sometimes Cat came over and helped or watched *Wheel of Fortune* while we worked. Grandma Melvyn smiled every time Cat yelled at the vowel people, but she kept working at the kitchen table instead of watching TV. She knew dozens of card tricks, and her sleight of hand was amazing, but she grumbled that she had lost her edge, so she worked even harder.

"We need something big," she said.

I liked the way she said "we," even if it was really her doing the planning. I suggested ideas, and she nodded and said they were great or interesting or "What's Trixie making for dinner?" but she never wrote any of my ideas down, so I don't think she meant it. (Except the dinner part.) And you know what? That was okay. Grandma Melvyn knew more about magic than I might ever know. For now, it was enough to learn from her.

She started telling me things about her life as a magician. The glamorous parts: Living in expensive hotels and performing for bigwigs at fancy nightclubs. The curtain calls and seeing her name in lights. The newspaper reporters and fan clubs. She also told me about the not-so-glamorous parts: Greasy food and sleeping on trains and buses and waking up in a different city every day. Though I'm not exactly sure what was bad about that. It sounded better than waking up each morning and going to the booger mines. And what's wrong with eating burgers and fries every night?

She told me about the handsome man whose smile had magically melted her heart and how they were supposed to get married. When she talked about him, she looked like maybe her heart was melting all over again. Then she'd crab at me because I was handling the cards all wrong or wasn't fast enough with my sleight of hand, or she'd yell at the nearest Trixie to tell them to stop doing whatever they were doing. It was her way of changing the subject. Grandma Melvyn was a magician, and she didn't want to be mushy. Nobody wants to hear a magician talk about their feelings.

Grandma Melvyn never told me about Trixie or the New Year's Eve that ended it all, and I didn't ask. I just listened. And maybe that was what she needed.

Besides, Grandma Melvyn and I were busy. Days flew by. Her operation was coming fast, and it was going to change everything. She'd have to stay in the hospital for two days, and when she came back, she would be in lots of pain.

I used to want Grandma Melvyn to go home more than anything in the universe (next to being a world-famous magician), but now it didn't seem so important to me. Or to Grandma Melvyn. I know she missed her house, but in a way, I think our house was her home now.

Anyway, there wasn't much time to think about it. There was lots to do, and the closer the operation came, the harder we worked.

CHAPTER 48

MOM TOOK GRANDMA MELVYN TO THE HOSPITAL FOR BLOOD TESTS THE DAY before her operation. It must have been exhausting, because Grandma Melvyn came home and went right to bed. I didn't even get a chance to wish her good luck on her operation or to give her the present I had made for her. And, no—it did not involve green glitter. It was a journal for her ideas. I wrote a note on the first page to wish her good luck and tucked the notebook and pen inside Grandma Melvyn's suitcase by the door. Mom and Grandma Melvyn were leaving the house before I got up for school in the morning. Her operation started at six thirty, but she had to be prepped for surgery before that.

I had a hard time paying attention at school. Well,

harder than usual. I spent most of the morning doodling ideas for a disappearing money trick. In the afternoon, I read my notes wrong and got an idea for a disappearing *monkey* trick, which was more fun to think about. By the way, if you know anyone with a monkey they'd like to loan out, I'm interested.

When school finally ended, I biked to the hospital, which was just beyond the drugstore where I got the cane and glitter. I popped inside the drugstore and bought a bag of peanut butter cups for Grandma Melvyn.

When I finally got to the hospital, the red-haired nurse at the main desk said Mom had already left, and I couldn't go to Grandma Melvyn's room without a badge, and those were only for adults. She said it with a go-away-and-stop-bothering-me-because-kids-don't-belong-here-and-you-are-really-annoying-me kind of look that made me mad.

I only wanted to say hello to Grandma Melvyn, but I couldn't do that because I wasn't old enough to vote? Why do grown-ups always assume kids will do something bad? What was I going to do? Cause a fire? Okay, bad example. But you know what I mean.

Lucky for me, there was a stack of visitor badges

sitting on the counter in front of the nurse. It was also lucky for me that there was a box of Kleenex on the counter behind her.

You know what else was lucky for me? That I was a fifth grader. Remember how I said that mucus was a fact of life in fifth grade? Well, you don't live through a fifth-grade cold season without learning a thing or two about sneezing. Besides, if you recall, I had a chance to witness all kinds of fake sneezes very recently, and I knew what worked and what didn't. See what I did there? I learned from my experience. That's what magicians do.

Anyway, I wasn't going to let a stupid rule keep me out.

"Excuse me," I said. "I'm going to . . . ah . . . ahhh . . . ahhhhhh—"

The nurse whipped around, grabbed a Kleenex from the box, and had it in my hand before I could say "—choo!"

"Tank-ooo," I said, blowing my nose. "Id derr a batroom?"

She pointed down the hall, and I followed her directions, holding the Kleenex to my nose with one hand and the bag of peanut butter cups with the other.

When she turned to help a doctor with a chart, I threw away the Kleenex, pulled the visitor pass from my jeans pocket, stuck it to my shirt, and ducked down the hall toward Grandma Melvyn's room.

CHAPTER 49

I HATED THE HOSPITAL. THE HALLWAY WAS TOO WARM AND THE LIGHTS WERE too bright and the smell was too clean. I suppose that it's good for a hospital to smell clean, but it made me queasy.

I finally found Grandma Melvyn's room. The door was cracked open just a little. I knocked on the metal door frame, but there was no answer. I waited a couple of seconds and knocked again. There was still no answer. Grandma Melvyn was probably asleep from painkillers, so I decided to leave the candy on her table and go home. I pushed the door open and peeked inside. It was a small room with only a hospital bed, a tiny table, and a dresser in the corner.

I expected Grandma Melvyn to be asleep with her

leg propped up, but she wasn't. Instead, she was sitting on the edge of her bed in her VIVA LAS VEGAS sweat suit, staring out the window.

"Grandma Melvyn?" I said.

She didn't move.

"It's Robbie," I said.

She sat still as stone. I stepped into the room and saw that her knee was not bandaged or wrapped up. She had not had the operation.

She stared blankly out the window, watching cars roll through the gate at the parking lot exit.

"How are—"

The red-haired nurse burst into the room.

"You're not supposed to be here!" she said. "Kids can only visit rooms with adults."

Grandma Melvyn whipped around and cast the Wicked Wobble Eye upon her.

"Am I adult enough for you, Trixie?" she asked.

"I . . . uh . . . ," the nurse stammered, backing out of the room and closing the door behind her.

Grandma Melvyn turned back to the window and stared blankly into the parking lot as if nothing had happened.

"I brought you some candy," I said.

I held up the bag of peanut butter cups, but Grandma Melvyn just kept staring out the window, so I put them on the tiny bedside table and stood there not knowing what to do next.

"Sit down," Grandma Melvyn finally said without looking at me.

There was only one place to sit in the room, so I sat on the bed next to her.

"Nice room," I said, even though it wasn't.

I don't think Grandma Melvyn even heard me, or if she did, she didn't care. She followed the cars with her eyes as they left the parking lot and drove down the road. I sat and watched them, too. Finally, she spoke, and her voice was almost a whisper.

"Why do people buy boring tan cars, Robbie?" she asked. "If they're trying to be invisible, it's not working. They're just wasting time."

Grandma Melvyn's voice told me that she wasn't looking for an answer, so I didn't say anything. I sat next to her and we watched the cars. Red. Red. Blue. Tan. Blue.

Finally, Grandma Melvyn took a deep breath and lifted her head and sat up straight.

"It's some trick, Robbie," she said. "Best I've seen."

"What trick?" I asked.

"Perfect misdirection," she said, "and I didn't I see it coming."

"What do you mean?" I asked.

"I'll show you," she said, pointing at her knee. "Ladies and gentlemen, here is an ordinary bum knee in need of an ordinary operation. Watch it closely . . . closely . . . First we schedule the operation and take some blood tests . . . Don't take your eyes off the knee . . . Watch it . . . Watch it . . . and . . ."

She tapped her index finger to her forehead.

"Ta-daaaa!" she said. "A tumor."

The word hit me like a bucket of ice water.

"What?" I asked.

"Didn't see it coming either, did you?" she asked. "Never know what a blood test will turn up."

She cleared her throat and tears welled up in her eyes.

"Some trick—" she said, but her words caught inside and tears rolled down her cheeks.

I didn't know what to do. I grabbed Grandma Melvyn's hand and squeezed it, and she squeezed back and held on tight like my hand was the only thing keeping her from being torn away by an invisible tornado that would toss her so far into the air she'd never find her way back again. We sat together long after the tornado had passed, and she found her breath again and hot tears filled my eyes and I blinked them away as we watched blurry cars roll out of the parking lot and drive away one by one. Some of them red and some of them blue and some of them tan.

"Wasted time," Grandma Melvyn whispered. "So much wasted time."

CHAPTER 50

GRANDMA MELVYN STAYED AT THE HOSPITAL FOR TWO DAYS WHILE THEY ran tests and took pictures of her brain and tried to figure out what they could do to fight the tumor inside her head. After the second day, they said they couldn't do much, but they should keep looking. She told them that they could look all they wanted, but she was going home.

She was sitting at the kitchen table, sketching in the notebook I'd given her, when I got home from school that Friday.

"Took you long enough," she said.

"I'm not the one who's been at the spa for two days," I said, pulling the pack of cards from the drawer and handing them to her.

"They ran out of chocolate, so I left," she said, shuffling cards and spreading them into a fan.

And that was all we said about Grandma Melvyn's time in the hospital. She had stuck around long enough to learn they couldn't do anything to stop the tumor or get rid of it, so she left. She had things to do.

In a way, leaving the hospital that way broke the rules of magic, like always knowing what's going to happen next and being prepared for it. On the other hand, sometimes you just have to smile and keep going even when you know the trick isn't going to work out the way you want. That's what Grandma Melvyn did. So that's what I did, too. Because what else are you going to do? Give up?

We worked every day after school until Grandma Melvyn got tired and had to sit in the chair and nap, which happened more and more. Sometimes her head hurt so much she took off her glasses and covered her eyes with a damp washcloth. She sat in the recliner with the TV on, and just when I thought she was sleeping, she'd yell at the vowel people. Sometimes she was too tired to do that, so I yelled for her. The bunch of Trixies.

And then one day she went back to the hospital. She didn't want me to visit, so I didn't. I could have. I could have gone with Mom or Dad, who came back from China. Or even with Aunt Trudy or Uncle Pete, who came back from their trip. Someone was always at the hospital with Grandma Melvyn. And even if they weren't, I could have stolen another pass and sneaked in if I'd wanted to. But she asked me not to, so I stayed home. Going to the hospital would have been like letting people come backstage after your final bow. Grandma Melvyn knew that never worked. People think they want to know how tricks work, but they don't. They want to believe in magic. Let them. Isn't that whole point?

And then one day, Mom came back from the hospital and before she said anything, I just knew.

"I'm sorry," Mom said, and even though I knew it was coming and I thought I was ready for it, I wasn't, and her words felt like an elephant crushing my chest.

My eyes burned and tears rolled down my cheeks, and I wanted to run far away and keep running, but I couldn't move; and then Mom wrapped her arms around me and pulled me close and we stood there in the kitchen hanging on to each other until our tears stopped, and then we stood there longer than that.

At last, Mom wiped her eyes and reached into her bag.

"She wanted you to have this," she said, and handed me the notebook I had given Grandma Melvyn. Mom kissed my cheek.

"Go ahead," she said.

I opened the notebook, looking and hoping for a note or message from Grandma Melvyn. Hoping to find one final lesson. I flipped through sketches covered with notes and spaghetti arrows and giant Xs and exclamation points. I flipped past thirty pages of rejected scribbles, and then there was nothing. The rest of the notebook was empty. Grandma Melvyn had stopped. There was no lesson for me. No advice. No note.

No good-bye.

And then I flipped the notebook over and I saw it. Taped to the back cover was a picture of me and Grandma Melvyn standing together under the lights of the Hobson Elementary School auditorium, taking our bow and smiling like the whole world was ours. And under the photograph was a single word written in Grandma Melvyn's chicken-scratch handwriting. Just one word that said it all. That said everything I needed to hear. Just one word.

Ta-daaaa!

CHAPTER 51

I STILL HAVE GRANDMA MELVYN'S NOTEBOOK, AND I USE IT TO DRAW MY OWN ideas for my act. I think she left most of the book empty so I could continue where she left off. And that's what I'm going to do. Cat has decided to learn magic, too, and I think she could become as good at it as me if she works hard enough. Grandma Melvyn would like that.

There's one more thing I want to tell you. I've been thinking a lot about that moment with no name when anything can happen. And I finally know what to call it.

It's *magic*.

I think Grandma Melvyn knew that, and now you do too.

There's not much left to do but say thanks for reading my book. I'll be in sixth grade next fall at Peterson Middle School, and I'll have a new act. I don't know what it is yet, but I can tell you one thing.

It's going to be magnificent.

KEEP READING FOR A
SNEAK PEEK OF
ANDREA BEATY'S

ATTACK
OF THE FLUFFY
BUNNIES

Chapter 1

Meanwhile, in space . . .

The flaming meteor hurtled through the endless, black void. Remember this. It's important later.

Chapter 2

Meanwhile, to begin our story . . .

Not long ago, in a galaxy just beyond the Milky Way—but not quite as far as the Peanut Cluster—there lived a race of fierce, large, ugly, and ferocious furballs known as the Fierce, Large, Ugly, and Ferocious Furballs. (Fluffs for short—though in reality, there is nothing short about Fluffs.)

In fact, Fluffs were (and are) tall with two enormous rabbitlike ears, two enormous rabbitlike feet, two enormous rabbitlike eyes, and one small rabbitlike nose. (Well, they couldn't have two noses. That would be weird.)

Okay, so the Fluffs are rabbits. But they are not mild-mannered, cute-cuddly-carrot-crunching, happy-hopping rabbits like those found on Earth. The Fluffs are fierce warrior rabbits whose long, floppy ears are for slapping. Whose long, floppy feet are for stomping. And whose large eyes spin in opposite directions to hypnotize unsuspecting prey. Oh yeah, and they have fangs.

For scientifically minded readers, a comparative study of Fluffs and domestic Earth rabbits is found on the next page in **Table 1: Know Your Fluff,** taken from *The Illustrated Guide to Fluffs and Other Space Creatures You Don't Want to Meet* by Professor Donald J. Dewdy. (Work unpublished.) Go ahead and take a moment to read it, if you want. The rest of us will meet you at the next chapter.

For nonscientifically minded readers, readers who wish they were playing video games right now (you know who you are), and readers forced to read this book for school book reports (so sorry), we'll sum up the contents of Table 1: FLUFFS = BAD.

Go to next chapter.

TABLE 1: KNOW YOUR FLUFF

	EARTH BUNNIES	FLUFFS
Genus	*Sylvilagus floridanus*	*Lepus fluffaricus*
Habitat	Woodlands, meadows, Saturday morning cartoons, pet shops	Fluffs inhabit hot-chocolate marshes on a series of extremely small planets in the Mallow Galaxy. The small, marshmallow-shaped planets have a sucrose-based core and are recognized by their spongy, white—and yummy—surfaces. At the center of the Mallow Galaxy is the Starburst, a large, orange cube-shaped star of sweet candy goodness. The Starburst's radiant energy fuels all life-forms within the Mallow Galaxy.
Diet	Grass, herbs, bunny chow, carrots	Diet? Are you kidding? Who could diet on a marshmallow planet? Fluffs absorb sugary energy through their fine, tubelike clear fur. Fluff fur appears silver-white, but is tinged with pink upon closer inspection. **(WARNING: Closer inspection of a Fluff can be hazardous to your health. Side effects may include but are not limited to: being eaten; being slapped by long, floppy, but surprisingly strong ears; being eaten; being stomped by long, floppy, but surprisingly strong feet; and being hypnotized by large and surprisingly swirly eyes, followed by being eaten.)**

	EARTH BUNNIES	FLUFFS
		Starburst energy supplies all required nutrients to the Fluffs, but they do enjoy the occasional snack when one presents itself (and is too slow, stupid, or spellbound by the Fluffs' swirly eyes to escape). Fluffs are, at present, the only known life-forms left in the Mallow Galaxy. Go figure.
Communication	Nose twitching, tail twitching, extreme cuteness	Mind waves. The hollow tubules of Fluff fur act as telepathic transmitters and receivers. Once transmitted, Fluff brain waves can travel long distances via sweet waves of sugary goodness emitted by the Starburst at the center of the Mallow Galaxy.
Predators	Coyotes, hawks, bob-cats, the Tasmanian Devil, and Elmer Fudd.	Predators? Are you asking what *eats* Fluffs? Ha ha ha ha ha ha ha ha ha ha ha ha ha ha ha ha ha ha . . . snort. . . . That's a good one.

Chapter 3

Remember the flaming meteor hurtling through space from Chapter 1? Here's an update.

Chapter 4

And then . . .

Chapter 5

"**What's that smell?**" thought Moopsy.*

"It wasn't me," thought Floopsy.*

"Smeller's the feller," thought Cottonswab.*

"Hey!!!" thought Moopsy.

The Fluffs looked at one another. They looked at the planet. They looked at one another again.

"Planet's on fire," thought Floopsy.

"So get a small creature and beat out the flames," thought Cottonswab.

"You ate the last small creature two years ago," thought Floopsy.

"Oh yeah," thought Cottonswab. "That reminds me . . . BUURP."

FWOOSH!

"Did you know burps were flammable?" thought Moopsy.

"EVACUATE!" thought Floopsy.

"EVACUATE!" thought Moopsy.

"BURP!" thought Cottonswab.

---

*Those of you who skipped Table 1 a few pages back might be wondering why these Fluffs seem to be thinking all the time instead of talking to each other. Hint: It's not because they are smart. This might be a good time for you to go back and read that table before it's too late. We'll take a nap while you read it. Wake us up when you get back.

Chapter 6

Meanwhile, on Earth . . .

The Rockman family van screeched to a halt in front of the crumbling stone arch at the entrance to Camp Whatsitooya. Through the arch, a gravel road wound its way into the dark woods, dwindled to two dirt tracks, and disappeared beyond a half-dead oak tree.

"Out, you two!" said Mr. Rockman. "Time for adventure!"

"Are you sure this is the place?" asked Kevin. "You can't even read that sign, it's old and cruddy and covered with moss or something."

"Of course it's the place," said Mrs. Rockman. "It says so right here on the map."

"And besides, it's not cruddy," said Mr. Rockman. "It's rustic. It says that right here in the brochure. We would never send you to a camp that called itself cruddy."

Mr. Rockman jumped out of the van, sprinted to the back hatch, tossed a mound of camping gear onto the road, sprinted back to the driver's seat, and buckled up again. All in 3.7 seconds flat.

"Yep! Yep! Yep!" said Mrs. Rockman, snapping her fingers excitedly. "We're here, darlings! Oh, summer camp! Beautiful summer camp! Swimming! Hiking! Campfires and marshmallows! I could linger here all day just breathing in the forest air. . . . Well, time's ticking. Off you go!"

Joules and Kevin Rockman climbed out of the van and stood in the ankle-high weeds at the edge of the road.

"Don't you want to come with us to check in?" asked Joules. "You know, just to make sure it's okay."

"Of course it's okay," said Mr. Rockman. "It says so in the brochure. See? 'Camp Whatsitooya, nestled on the aromatic shores of Lake Whatsosmelly. Camp Whatsitooya: Exceptionally Exceptional Outdoors Experiences Guaranteed. No Exceptions.*'"

Joules and Kevin groaned. What kind of person would write that stuff?

"And they have a spa," said Mrs. Rockman. "See? There's even a picture!"

---

*Possible exceptions include, but are not limited to, poison oak, poison ivy, ivy league, little league, 20,000 leagues under the sea, sea sickness, seesaws, spider bite, snake bite, trilobite, and overbite. Results may vary. Guarantee not valid in Illinois, Kentucky, Pennsylvania, or any other state.

"It's an outhouse," said Joules.

"It's rustic!" said her mother. "What could be better?"

Joules and Kevin could each think of at least four hundred and seven thousand things that would be better, but they knew it was pointless to argue, so they simply shrugged.

"Well, my dears, we simply must go," said Mrs. Rockman. "Those Cherry-Cheese SPAMcakes won't cook themselves! Wish us luck!"

Mr. and Mrs. Rockman were on their way to the International SPAMathon in Cheekville, Pennsylvania. The Rockmans loved SPAM, that somewhat pickled, highly pink, and frighteningly brick-shaped canned meat substance used by the army in World War II as food for soldiers and/or construction material and/or a convenient object to stuff in a cannon if needed.

Every summer, Mr. and Mrs. Rockman competed in the International SPAMathon Dessert Competition. And lost. Until last year, when Mrs. Rockman's Funky-Chunky-Chocolate SPAM Pudding captured the judges' hearts and intestinal tracts. The Rockmans were crowned SPAM King and SPAM Queen and invited back this year to defend their crowns.

Unlike their parents, Joules and Kevin did not love SPAM festivals. They thought SPAM was all right, but their parents' recipes were all wrong. So very, *very* wrong. Joules and Kevin had jumped at the chance to go to camp instead of this year's Festival of Chunky Funkiness, as they called it. What could be better than a week of swimming and hiking and eating marshmallows? But as they stood in the weeds and looked past the crumbling stone arch into the dark forest of Camp Whatsitooya, they had second thoughts.

And third thoughts.

And fourth thoughts.

"But what if something goes wrong?" asked Kevin.

"What could possibly go wrong?" asked Mrs. Rockman, blowing them a kiss as Mr. Rockman hit the gas. The squeal of tires echoed through the trees like the cry of a wounded cat.

"Famous Last Words," said Joules as she watched the family van grow smaller and smaller in the distance.

"Yep," said Kevin.

"You know what that means," said Joules.

"Yep," said Kevin.

"I hate Famous Last Words," said Joules.

"Yep," said Kevin.

Joules and Kevin Rockman shouldered their gear and headed through the crumbling stone arch into the deep woods of Camp Whatsitooya.

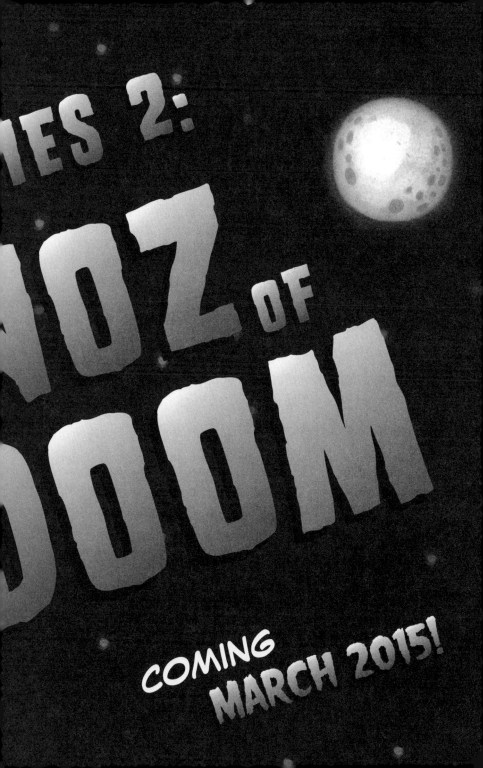

ABOUT THE AUTHOR

ANDREA BEATY, OTHERWISE KNOWN AS ANDREA THE AMAZING, IS THE AUTHOR of many spellbinding, spectacular books for young people, including *Secrets of the Cicada Summer* and *Attack of the Fluffy Bunnies*, both of which appeared on the master list of Florida's Sunshine State Young Readers Award. She is also the author of the picture books *When Giants Come to Play; Iggy Peck, Architect; Rosie Revere, Engineer;* and *Happy Birthday, Madame Chapeau*. Andrea often visits schools to teach students the magic of writing. Learn more about her programs and her books at andreabeaty.com.